D1297592

the Silent rooms

Also by Anne Hébert

Kamouraska

the Silent rooms

a novel by
ANNE HÉBERT

translated by
Kathy Mezei

Musson Book Company
Don Mills, Ontario

First published as *Les Chambres de bois*
Original French edition © 1958 by Editions du Seuil
English translation © 1974 by Musson Book Company

First published in 1974 by
Musson Book Company,
30 Lesmill Road, Don Mills, Ontario

ISBN 0-7737-0020-X
Printed and bound in Canada
1 2 3 4 5   BP   79 78 77 76 75 74

the
Silent
rooms

PART ONE

Catherine's home was in a town where blast furnaces flamed in the sky, day and night, like the dark palaces of the Apocalypse. In the morning, women wiped their windows, blackened by the fierce fires of the night.

Catherine's windows were spotless and the tiles of the kitchen floor gleamed like the black and white squares of a beautiful chessboard. Her home was always sparkling, for Catherine never let work or time overwhelm her. Since the death of her mother, were there not three younger sisters to be fed, bathed, combed, dressed, and their clothes mended while their father retreated into solitude?

The year of her mother's death, summer was so hot and black that soot dripped from every pore. The blast furnaces blazed in furious competition with the fires of summer. Bread was plentiful but hard-won, and women complained softly against the sooty faces of men quick with desire.

The countryside nearby was steaming like a stagnant pool. When autumn came, Catherine and her sisters were taken there, to visit an elderly uncle who no longer worked. His house was a shambles, since there was no one to do the chores. The little girls ran all the errands for their uncle, who had invited them for this reason.

Then, one day, on their way to the village, they became lost in the fog. All the paths looked the same, crossing canals, running along the edge of meadows where wispy trees stood, blue with mist, repeated here and there like a motif.

The youngest sister started to cry. Catherine held her hand tightly, and stubbornly continued on through the wet fields, searching for a shop selling wine, tobacco and materials for repairing a broken armchair. Soon the rain was pouring down with such fury that all four huddled beneath a tree, heads lowered, cheek to cheek, arms around each other and backs to the storm, bound together in a thick sheaf of lost children. Catherine peered through the tangles of her hair, her lashes brushing Lucie's cheek. Lucie tossed her head, as if shaking off a fly. Her eyes followed Catherine's and they both saw the hunter and the children emerge from the woods.

The man strode along in front. Close on his heels followed a girl struggling to walk quickly in spite of the gun slung across her shoulders. A boy trailed behind, his head bent, bowed under the weight of the game bag.

It was Lucie who asked for directions. The man answered shortly, bored. Then, as he looked at Lucie, an expression of quickening interest and craftiness flashed over his languid face, as if a fox had suddenly dropped his mask. He murmured to Lucie that he found her promising for her age and pointed out the way to the village. Then he resumed his bored and arrogant air.

They all remained a few minutes longer under the shelter of the trees in the falling rain, the children a little apart from their father.

The face of the hunter's daughter was the colour of nutmeg, with narrow and intense black eyes slanting up towards her temples. Without looking at Catherine and her sisters, she said stiffly that she had been hunting in the marshes since before daybreak and that the game bag was full of quail. The little boy said he had a fever. He raised his frightened, tearful face to Catherine, adding in a whisper that his father was making him carry the heavy bag of wounded birds. Catherine was so close to him that she could have traced the path of his tears with her finger as they trickled down his bony cheeks. An acrid smell of bloody game emanated from the boy, like the odour of his own misery.

The hunter whistled to his hounds, and started on his way, at his heels the girl, the boy and the long, lean dogs.

That evening, Lucie goaded her uncle into speech, although he preferred above all else to be silent, as if he hoped to become a smooth, worn wall, or a mute stone, or a scowling corpse. Watching her uncle through her lashes, Lucie told him about the hunter who had found her promising for her age.

As her words forced their way through the uncle's silence, the veins swelled in his neck and at his temples. He swore, choked, and then, half in resentment, half in bitter mirth, he spoke about the usurpation of hunting and fishing rights, about the way the entire countryside had been ravaged by one *seigneur*, wounded animals left rotting in the brush and reckless young girls ruined in a night. He described the squat house with its long, narrow windows. Lowering his voice, he told them about the woman who lived there in perpetual idleness, frequently resorting to ostentation and cruelty. He himself had seen her motionless owl's face, silhouetted against the window of the seigniorial manor one rainy evening.

After they had laid in stores of wine, tobacco, kindling, flour, sugar and salt, and when the ancient cuckoo clock had begun to chime the correct hour, when the creaking hinges were silenced with oil, and everything was spic and span and the dog no longer roamed wild, the uncle sent his nieces home.

Catherine and her sisters never returned to the country.

Long afterwards, a landscape drowned in rain and fog continued to haunt the little girls, one or the other and sometimes all of them at once. And then, in the evenings after their father had fallen asleep, they exchanged their impressions in hushed voices. The two beds touched in the shadows, forming a single field of sleeping sisters, Lucie's head a black cluster amid the loose, bleached straw of the other's entangled hair.

Catherine, the oldest, exercising the privilege of age, stored the vision of the seigniorial manor deep in her heart along with other sombre and sacred objects – such as the death of her mother, and her own interrupted childhood. She dreamt:

"On the top shelf of the cupboard among orderly piles of linen, the seigniorial manor lay in the hollow of a glass ball, like a ship in a bottle. The perfume of trees was captured there and the endless misery of a little boy, bereft of all compassion. When Catherine seized the glass ball in her hands, rain and fog fell, slowly, upon the manor, the trees and the child's misery. As if an hourglass had been inverted, the entire image was washed away."

But the day beckoned to Catherine. There were mornings filled with the fragrance of little girls, their shrill voices tearing at one another like claws and the interweaving of golden and jet-black curls. Now and then, the rarely heard voice of their father would ring out, a dull gong demanding silence.

When the father was at work and the sisters at school, Catherine bent her innocent head over the day's tasks. Everything ran very smoothly, as if this child's hands were two competent servants forced to struggle alone and endlessly all their harsh life against the blackness of the land, and the malignant dampness that clung to the linen, the furniture, the corners of the house, the father's heavy boots, and even to the bitter lines of his face.

One winter was so cold that Catherine's ivy shrivelled against the windowpane. Snow covered the countryside. The silence was so deep that year that you could actually hear the pulse of life. Gradually, the sooty footprints in front of the doors were wiped away. For two whole days they were without wood. The youngest child had a fever and wept from a sharp pain in her side. The father, in a state of mute fury, was happy to shut himself in for long periods.

By the time the winter ended, Lucie was taller than Catherine. In the first sunlight of spring, she stood at the doorway, stretching with the quiet joy of a girl who has shed her childhood. Her youngest sister perched on her shoulders, she went for a long walk along the rough, uneven streets. All over town, people were muttering anxiously that work, which had previously sought out men, was now letting them go, one by one. High upon her sister's shoulders, the little girl caught a glimpse through a window of a man without work stretched across his bed in broad daylight like a punished child, staring bitterly at the ceiling.

It occurred to Lucie that her father was growing old and that his age was endangering the security of their home. The same evening, she announced abruptly that she didn't want to go to school any more and that she, instead of Catherine, would do the housekeeping.

She cut off her long braids and brought them to her father. Confronted by rebellion for the first time, by a bobbed head, by a child with her forehead set as if she were about to ram it against a stone wall, the man seized her long black braids and, wielding them like a couple of horsewhips, slashed her across the face.

The father had a sister called Anita. One day she arrived, sniffed her nieces like a bouquet of flowers and found them fresh and lovely. When she was informed of the problems of the household, her face grew intense and preoccupied, with the look of someone trying to thread a needle. First of all she assured the father that a man loses his capacity to work only if he allows it to happen. As for her nieces, she felt that the eldest one should be married off and the younger take her place in the household. She despaired of Catherine's childish figure. And what a pity that the girl's profile looked so grave as she bent over her sewing by the window.

From that time on, at the hour when flames from the blast furnaces battled with the violet light of the long summer evenings, Catherine could be found sitting on her doorstep.

The men of the region were rough and wild, and the pale girl with her too short skirts and bony knees would pretend to be working or affect a childish air whenever one of them stopped to look at her and wish her good evening. She wanted to nurture her dream and remain aloof, as defiant and mysterious as a woman secretly in pursuit of a barbarian prince.

In the hall of the deserted schoolhouse, Catherine paused among the tall green ferns to listen to the music. "The piano's in tune," she marvelled all the way along the corridor, as if at the sudden and overwhelming concord of all earthly things. "That's for the fête on Sunday," the headmistress had told her, trying to force the worn lines of her face into a smile.

Catherine sat down near the piano, fascinated by the visible flow of music to the pianist's fingers and to his strange and agitated face. "No one is listening but me," she thought, rather frightened by the intensity of her absorption. The stranger was playing for her. Soon she began to feel uneasy, for the music was racing, becoming frantic, like rice leaping above the fire.

Then the young man stopped playing. He came towards Catherine. She saw the olive tone of his skin, the fineness of his bones and the astonishing almond-eyed gaze, watching guardedly from under his eyelashes, occasionally flashing over her like a blaze of gold.

It was as if he wanted to protect his fingers from any contact. Catherine despised such delicate hands. He sat down on the bench beside her, looking at her without seeing her, admitting his weariness, the ebbing of that exaltation which had seized him at the piano like a storm. Footsteps sounded in the corridor. The young man stood up. He whispered in Catherine's ear, "One day I'll give a real recital, in a real concert hall – you'll see . . ."

He bowed to Catherine as if concluding a concert performance. He made her promise to come to the school fête because he wished to see her again.

Catherine had to race after her younger sisters, who had already left the school.

The following Sunday, the day of the concert, they waited a long time for the pianist, but he never appeared. The audience was buzzing with restless children, so at the request of the headmistress, a lady with red hair played the violin and two skinny little girls danced a flamenco.

After the performance, Catherine went home with her sisters. They discussed the pianist, who lived in the country, near the forest in a house as big as the school.

"That's the countryside we visited the year mother died," said Catherine.

She was careful not to mention her encounter with the pianist to her sisters, wondering quietly to herself why he hadn't come to the concert. A land of mist and forest rose before her. Once again she was meeting an arrogant *seigneur* in hunting boots and a dark girl, as prickly as a cactus, and then the image of a terrified little boy came into focus and took on the shape of a man.

One morning the mailman handed Catherine a letter. He insisted it was for her. She was alone in the house, doing the laundry, a thick braid of hair flapping at her back. Wiping her hands, she turned the letter over and over before she made up her mind to open it.

The letter was signed "Michel". It read: "I don't know your name. I know nothing about you. I found out where you live by following you that other night without your knowing. Forget about that concert I missed through ill-fortune. And please come this evening at the agreed time to that place near the school by the trees in the park as if I was asking you for the first time."

In the park, with its gnarled trees and sooty lanes, Michel and Catherine sat down on some shaky, rusty chairs. They could hear the muffled sounds of the town, far off in the distance. The wind had quieted down. Yellow leaves fell at almost regular intervals, like coins dropped into a pool. Michel watched Catherine furtively, without speaking. When she got up to leave, he tried to detain her. "You'll come again, won't you? I'll wait for you here, at the same time."

She nodded, tossing her hair. The young man clasped her hand, red and wrinkled by water. She quickly pulled herself away and ran home.

About this time Anita started to come almost daily. Her laughter could be heard mingling with the children's in the evening around dinner time. Everyone tried to outdo the other, to help, protect and arrange for Catherine's rendezvous with Michel without the father's finding out. When Catherine arrived home, silence fell. In defiance, she also said nothing.

Who had told Anita about Michel? Hadn't Catherine always lifted a blank and unresponsive face towards her aunt in reply to all her probings?

However, Michel never again turned up at the rendezvous and every evening Catherine pretended to her sisters and Anita that she had to meet the young, handsome, and idle *seigneur* at his pressing invitation. She would go for walks along the streets all by herself, gazing at the display windows and shops, choosing flowers, dresses and jewels, not in the least deceived by her own frail image reflected in the store windows as she passed.

Then one evening, while Catherine lingered in the park before returning home, Michel was once again in front of her, greeting her as easily as if he had never left her.

They walked together by the edge of the canal.

He said he had come through the woods, which were already deep with shadows under their umbrella of trees. Catherine replied that she had to go home, that they were all waiting for her. She spoke quietly, watching the young man furtively, not daring to question him about his long absence. Inwardly, she wondered: "Who made him forget me so easily, for so many days, as if I'd died long ago?

What peculiar seigniorial duty kept him at home, prevented him from coming to me?" And she searched his freshly shaven face in vain for some sign of tragedy or illness or fever. "How calm and distant and collected he appears," she thought. And suddenly, it seemed to her that someone wanted to cleanse her heart of a shining and fabulous childhood château, imprisoned in a land of rain and fog.

Michel's voice at her ear startled her. "What are you thinking about, Catherine? You're very quiet."

"Nothing, Michel, nothing ..."

"Isn't it beautiful and calm this evening? I believe I haven't felt so peaceful in a long time."

Catherine repeated that she wanted to go home. Michel looked surprised, then became agitated, as if fearful of losing her.

"But Catherine, I've hardly seen you and already you want to leave me."

Catherine felt Michel's anguish weighing down upon her like a restraining hand. But she hid the joy this gave her.

Michel came the next day and all the following days. As soon as he neared the town, his eyes sought out Catherine, quite oblivious of the passersby. He tramped along the pavement with long strides as if he were still in the forest, excitedly skirting the marshes, among the grass and branches, startling waterfowl as he passed.

Wherever Catherine went in the town, there was always an hour between the day and the autumn night when the young man would come bounding up to her, his boots muddy, a lean hound at his heels.

Catherine became frightened. She begged Michel to be cautious so that they wouldn't be seen in town together. She described her strict home, where a taciturn man sat every evening among his daughters. And suddenly the fleeting and silent shadow of Anita slipped into Catherine's heart and her heart contracted.

How oppressive this house seems under its weight of sleep, thought Catherine as she tucked in her sleeping sisters. She quickly got undressed. But, disturbed by Anita's belated presence in the living room, she was reluctant to go to bed.

"What's keeping her from going home? She never leaves home without her eyes carefully made up, without some design painted on her set face. Ever since dinner, she's been fussing over me. She points at the mud on my shoes. She analyzes my every expression, is surprised if I sing, makes a big fuss about a paltry yellow leaf stuck to my sweater. She does everything but sniff my hands to track down that wild scent that captures my heart so swiftly, so surely that I'll not be able to sleep for a long time."

Twice Anita's muffled voice called Catherine. Anita knew very well that she wouldn't be able to draw a word, gesture or glance from this guarded, stony girl. "But her heart is beating under there, stung to the quick by my words, as if pricked by thorns."

Anita explained that Michel's great wealth would provide an eternity of leisure for him. She also spoke of Catherine's father who was nearing the end of his working days, and didn't know what to do with four daughters still at home. She dwelt upon the humiliation of this man whose only resource was anger. She spoke in hushed tones, her head bent towards Catherine, searching her eyes, biting off each word.

"Catherine, you know you've been seen together in town, you and Michel. One of these days your father will find out about it. What is there between this boy and you? Not a great deal, I expect, you innocent child. But you know your father doesn't take love or death lightly. Are you at least listening to me, Catherine?"

At this point, the father muttered confusedly in his sleep. Catherine jumped.

Anita sat back and said very quietly, almost regretfully, "You must get married, Catherine . . ."

The young girl swallowed painfully, as if she were choking. "To Michel?"

"To Michel? Of course, who else?"

The father let out an inhuman cry. He was complaining violently about a terrible, rusty weathercock creaking through the town, calling the dead. Then, in his normal voice he first asked, then pleaded that they close all the doors and windows tightly.

Catherine stepped up to her aunt, whose hand was already on the latch. Her blue eyes widened enormously. She murmured in a whisper, "Aunt Anita, I'm afraid that this is all a dream and Michel will never marry me."

When Catherine told Michel she remembered him as a small boy, he was surprised and his face darkened. He replied that he didn't recall the meeting and, besides, he didn't like to be reminded of the past. Catherine continued, describing the rain, her sisters, the hunter and his children. Michel seemed bored by Catherine's story. Then, he suddenly turned towards her, staring straight into her eyes with his sharp, yellow gaze.

"Ah! Catherine, who revives the past? I was feeling as comfortable with you as if I'd never had a childhood."

Catherine stared fixedly at two pebbles by her feet.

"Michel, I want to know. I've got to know. What goes on in your home and in the forest around? What happens to you when you leave town? I want to know, Michel! And that dark sister of yours?"

"That little sister, Catherine, so dark, so violent, so young and almost damned . . . But what do you mean by this? Do I ask questions about your home?"

He raised her head. Holding it between his hands, close to him, he smoothed back her hair, stroked her hard little skull, touching her forehead, her nose, her chin, her tear-dampened cheeks, like someone savouring the cool hardness of a pebble polished by the sea. Catherine stared back at him for a long time, without lowering her eyes, and Michel began to tremble as if he were afraid.

For three days, Catherine refused to go out at her customary time. She forbade the children to leave the house. She ordered the shutters and door closed earlier, using as a pretext the fog and that earthy smell that pervaded the town with the descent of the long autumn evenings. When their father came home, he seemed comforted by the closeness of the house.

The fourth evening, Catherine went to bed while Lucie took charge of the house. A chorus of alternating childish voices bombarded Catherine's half-sleep, mingling with the voice of that sombre enchantment deep inside her.

"Why does Catherine forbid us to go out? – It's

Michel who makes her as nasty as poison ivy! – Is Catherine going to marry Michel? – I don't want him to take her away to that house in the depths of the woods! – You go inside and it smells of cedar chests and damp ferns. You can get lost in that steaming city of a kitchen, cluttered with spices, cooking smells, dazzling copper pots and pans. – The women, especially, are evil and they sleep in the farthest rooms in beds as big as houses."

During the last few seconds, Lucie's voice kept rising, solitary, intoxicated by her own words. Catherine, now wide awake, had got up to listen to her sister's story.

"The mother died, all alone, during the early morning hours. The children asleep by the fire didn't notice. Their servant had fled away the night before and their father hadn't come back from hunting. Then he died in a foreign land. The little girl grew up. It's a house ruled by women. She has engraved her name on the windows and mirrors. Lia, that's her name, the sister of Michel . . ."

Catherine turned upon Lucie.

"It's not true. It's not true. You're making up stories to frighten the children. Only I have the right to talk about Michel and his house. Who told you all this?"

"Everyone in town talks about it. And they talk about you too, a silly little fool chasing after the nobility."

Very early the next morning, even before they had opened up the house, Anita was knocking at the door. Her voice was shrill and insinuating.

"I found two dead leaves, golden, perfectly shaped, on your doorstep, the size of a hand and flat as water-lilies."

She handed the leaves to Catherine. No one noticed the letter that lay hidden between them.

"I never see you any more, Catherine. Is it possible I've lost you? Come quickly, the garden will die any day now, battered by wind and ice. Let it be as you wish. If you come (and you shall, for I'm begging you) I'll receive you into that world of my childhood, which you've already entered without my realizing it. Do come, Catherine, here nothing's changed (in appearance), neither the garden nor the house. All I do is wait for you. Michel."

Anita left the door open. "It's mild, Catherine, let the sun in."

"How can I visit Michel?" Catherine wondered. "Take that long trip without father finding out?"

Anita handed various things to Catherine across the table.

"Here's a necklace and this big, embroidered shawl that belonged to your mother."

Catherine didn't dare touch anything. Suddenly, she inhaled a whiff of iris that pierced her heart. She buried her head in the shawl and began nibbling it so her mother's scent would enter her mouth and touch her teeth, her palate.

Anita stood in front of Catherine, humbled and hurt by the child's passion. She thought, "Little one, little one, how warm and eager you are, and I'm a woman whose account is settled. Nothing more will happen to me and so I have nothing to teach you . . ."

"Aunt Anita, how can I get to Michel's?"

The father never went out unless there was an occasion to revive his own long-standing grief. That evening he announced that he would spend the night keeping vigil over a young woman who had died, the wife of a companion at work.

As soon as he had left, Catherine got into the car beside Anita. Neither the paved road nor the pruned woods seemed familiar. When they came in view of the house, she was surprised to have arrived so soon and bewildered by the absence of turrets, balconies and barred windows. The garden seemed small and untidy. Anita let her out and she stood alone for a moment by the iron gate until the ringing of the rusty bell subsided. The stone house lay there, massive, its closed windows barred against the light.

Soon Michel appeared, walking warily over the sandy lane as if avoiding puddles. He hesitated before opening up the gate, seeming not to recognize Catherine.

"It's me, Michel," she murmured.

By now she detested the shawl, which was hampering her movements. Michel opened the gate, let the girl in and closed it behind her. He repeated, "It's you, Catherine," then was at a loss for words.

The sun was beginning to set, the garden scents were turning acrid. Something stirred near one of the windows. Michel started.

"Let's not stay here, Catherine; come, I'll show you the garden."

He skirted the house, leading Catherine right to the end of the garden. Then he leaned on the stone wall, staring up at a window on the first floor where a light had just been switched on. Suddenly he turned abruptly towards Catherine.

"Catherine, you can be seen from there! Bend down! Good! Like this, behind the hazel-bushes."

He knelt beside her, his head raised towards the window, perfectly still, alert, an animal on the watch.

Catherine pulled off her shawl with brief rapid movements of her hands and arms, brushing Michel's shoulder without his appearing to notice. She felt like crying out, like breaking the dry branches. She could hear each beat of Michel's heart while the fierce breath of the autumn earth and the soaked leaves flooded her nostrils. "It's like eating rotting grass!" she thought.

She shook her starched skirt and it crackled. She thought of her scratched legs. At her side, Michel did not move, fascinated by that solitary window shining in the night. Then someone up at the house closed the creaking shutters. Michel stood up and signalled Catherine to follow him.

Catherine couldn't tear her eyes away from that queer, massive dwelling which the night had now reclaimed. She thought the elusive heart of the earth might be buried there, along with Michel's piano, his palette of oils, his melancholy idleness and the whole life of the château. She recalled those cruel, idle women of noble lineage, now lying in their chalky bones, and suddenly the sharp vivid features of Lia, Michel's sister, rose up in her heart.

Michel called in a whisper, "Come quickly, Catherine, please."

He opened the closed iron gate very cautiously, holding the bell in his hand.

"Nothing in the world will make me look back," Catherine repeated to herself as the house receded in the distance, that house into which she had not been invited. She swore never to see Michel again, steeling herself as if afraid of being turned into a statue of salt at the least sign of regret. The silence was broken only by the steady sound of their footsteps on the road. The dark countryside began to terrify her. She drew nearer to Michel, casting fleeting glances at his face, obscured by the darkness. Michel started to speak, first in a whisper, then more loudly.

"Driven out! I'm driven out of my own house by shame! I'll never return there now. It's all filthy and wasted and ruined . . ."

Catherine's dull voice seemed to echo his meaningless words. "What do you mean, Michel? What is wasted and filthy and ruined?"

"Filth, that's what she's become, that most inviolable of all girls. She has brought evil upon us."

Michel's manner of speaking troubled Catherine like the flaunting of a wound. In her tiny colourless voice, she murmured, "Who has hurt you, Michel? Who has done this?"

Michel's words were almost inaudible and for the first time he seemed to be speaking to Catherine.

"Lia came back this evening and that man, her lover, is with her."

When they reached the town, Catherine wanted to part from Michel quickly so no one would see them together. He tried to hold her back, repeating that he was "all alone and miserable". She wheeled around like a small, pale, scathing rooster.

"And me, Michel?"

"You, Catherine? But what's wrong with you?"

"Nothing, nothing. I'm just caught in a trap like a mouse."

She forbade him to try to see her again, warning of her father's anger. Michel was astonished. He spoke hesitantly as if he didn't quite know what he was saying: "But Catherine, you're too small for anyone to hurt you."

She ran off towards her home.

He caught her at the doorstep, just as she was going in. A light shone in the living-room window.

He begged her to listen to him. He spoke of the loneliness of the stony town, of the wind on the square, of the man without home or friends, of the passionate blood of girls who are damned.

They were now standing beneath the neighbour's dark, shuttered windows. Michel was whispering his strange words against Catherine's face. She stood silent, turned towards the wall. "He talks and breathes on me like someone warming his fingers," she thought. Soon she no longer heard anything, conscious only of that moist warmth against her neck, her cheek. "I'm feeling dizzy," she thought.

Someone stirred in her father's house. Catherine edged nervously away, wanting to escape. Michel barred her way.

"Don't leave me, Catherine," he stammered. "I've no one but you now." He spoke feverishly, his fingers gripping her wrists.

"Stay with me, Catherine, I'll take you to Paris, to the apartment Lia and I keep for the concert season. I'll run away from her and that man."

The door of the house swung open. Lucie called out, "Is that you, Catherine?"

"I must go . . . I must go," she breathed, trying to free her wrists.

"Catherine, stay, please, don't leave me all by

myself. I'll ask your father for your hand if I must, but don't leave me all alone."

He had articulated this final, astonishing speech slowly, each word visibly bringing him immense peace.

Now his calm hands were caressing Catherine's neck, her waist, her throat, her face. It was as if he wanted to create, without haste or passion, a body that was soft and solid in the night.

PART TWO

To begin with, there was a full day in Michel's apartment, a crowded and clamorous day amid suit-cases, cartons, dust, last year's accumulated chaos, the comings and goings of the movers, bitter cold coffee and stale sandwiches, a fire that wouldn't start and the musty odour of closed rooms. Mingling with all this was the long wait for the night, the anguish of a night that is bound to come and is anticipated half-heartedly, like a sad train in a deserted station.

Catherine lay down in Michel's narrow, school-boy's bed. She switched off the lamp while a voice murmured humbly, fading away, "Good night,

Catherine, sleep well, little girl, I'll be sitting up in the next room."

And Catherine did not move, intent on the slow retreat of her husband's steps.

It was broad daylight when she awoke. She kept her eyes closed for awhile, first mapping out with her fingers the nearest signs of her new life; the eyelets embroidered on the sheets and, on the night table within reach of her hand, the delicate, smooth ring that a man in a dream had slipped on her finger.

But at once she began thinking about coffee, a grinder, matches, milk, cups, bread, butter, plates and knives, and she dressed hurriedly.

When she entered the large kitchen, which was used as a dining room as well, she saw Michel. He was asleep, rolled up in a blanket on a small, low couch that sagged like a broken step.

She knelt by the couch and called to him softly, disconcerted by the closeness of this nocturnal mask of a face. She called several times, louder and louder. The sound of her voice died away, then seemed to hit Michel on the rebound, like a slingshot. He started, but did not awake. She shook his shoulder, uncovering his chest in its defenceless nakedness. He moaned in his sleep, a rending, sensual sound. Catherine dropped her head onto the heart of this man, who had surrendered to desire and anguish in his dream.

She then inspected the apartment. It was in a complete jumble, as if cartloads of furniture and odd objects had been hastily thrown there by mad-men.

She started tidying up, trying not to disturb the silence. Suddenly, Michel stood before her, his face like a sleepwalker's, streaked by the bright light of noon. In a faint voice he asked for some coffee and insisted that Catherine draw the curtains.

He drank his coffee, smoked a cigarette, stretched, luxuriating in the dim light filtering through the closed curtains. Then he looked about for Catherine, calling her loudly.

"Catherine, where are you? What are you doing? I don't see you."

"Here, Michel, I'm here."

"I don't want you to work. That's the servant's job."

"And me, what am I going to do?"

Catherine stood very still, her arms dangling. Michel asked for more coffee.

There were many more such days and nights. The night unleashed anguish upon Michel like a savage bitch kept chained all day. And his days, half drowned in sleep, slipped by, mute, blind.

But there was an hour at twilight when he appeared before his wife, liberated from his abstractedness and fear, his face clear and beautiful, his hands free and compassionate. Then he loved to caress Catherine's arms and shoulders. He would freeze for a moment, his features drawn, his long lids shut and she would think, "I'm bound to him, but please God, let him take me without hurting me." But soon, all his warmth ebbed away. Catherine remained in his arms, abandoned, like a sacrificial maiden on a stone altar.

In the evenings, she stayed alone in the darkness while Michel sat at the piano in a distant corner of the room behind a straw screen, playing quietly. Only when Catherine was asleep did he light the lamp. Just before dawn he went to sleep in the kitchen.

One night, Catherine dreamt that Michel set out towards her. He never succeeded in reaching her. He travelled down one raging river after the other, until suddenly they all merged together with a tremendous roar. Awakening with a start, Catherine heard the strident chords of the piano, followed by the sound of shattering glass. Michel's profile was visible through the straw screen, like the face of some unknown man glimpsed behind the curtains of a stranger's window. She called his name. No reply. Just that motionless, bent shadow. She ran to the piano. There were splinters of glass on the floor and on the keyboard.

"Go to sleep, Catherine, you see its's nothing. I've broken a glass." Michel was forcing himself to speak calmly, deliberately, slowly. When she didn't move, he wheeled around and shouted: "Go away, Catherine! What are you doing, running around barefoot? Please go back to sleep. Don't I have the right any more to some solitude, to my own life?"

Catherine returned to her bed. A door slammed and Michel went to sleep in the next room, throwing himself on the couch, still fully clothed.

In the morning, Catherine let her mind linger over images of that black land where furnaces flamed in the sky, day and night. She thought for a long time of the shame she shared with Michel, of being able to sleep at leisure, without ever wanting bread. And she contemplated her white hands and her nails, that were lengthening like the claws of a captive animal.

Winter drizzled down over the city.

When Catherine leaned out the window that overlooked a courtyard deep and narrow as a well, her face and hands momentarily reflected pale mother-of-pearl and oyster colours like a mirror of water.

Michel came suddenly to life. He dreamt of combining Catherine's pallor with the beauty of the city, like the intricate blending of light and water.

"Come, Catherine, I want to do my palette over in your colours, the way they ought to be."

He began to strip off the dried paint with energetic strokes of his spatula, then made up a palette that was cool as a moist beach – sky, water, sand, pearl and sea-shells. Catherine gazed for a long time at the palette he held up to her, supposedly in her own colours.

"What are you thinking about, Catherine?"

"Nothing, Michel, your palette is beautiful, but I'm not sure I can look like that all the time."

He assured her that she had not stopped looking like her own reflection. He promised to go with her to the shops and buy every lovely thing that might suit her.

When the rain streamed down the grey window-panes all day long, Catherine sometimes shouted to Michel in a harsh voice alien to this calm, damp land, "I want to run till I'm breathless, barefoot through the puddles, with my youngest sisters, barefoot through the puddles, barefoot, do you hear, Michel?"

He always looked at her severely and asked her not to raise her voice.

Catherine already had several marvellous dresses, some fine lingerie, and strange and delicate jewelry. Michel had also given her a chair with a high, carved back and a huge bed of dark wood.

He had taken back his narrow iron cot and placed it near the piano behind the screen. Here he had a little house of straw for the night. He lit the lamp only when Catherine was asleep. When she happened to wake in the middle of the night, she would see, as in a dream, a strange straw hut set up in the corner of her room and the shadow of a man bent over music that had often just failed his fingers.

One evening, while tucking Catherine into bed, Michel pulled off her long nightgown. Her slender body with its barely rounded breasts and hips seemed nicely shaped to him. He hadn't counted on the softness of her skin beneath his fingers or the warmth of this adolescent body in his clumsy arms. "You're warm, Catherine," he stammered, "so soft and warm..."

He moved his trembling, icy hands over her body. He dreamt of exorcising this tender flesh. In a scarcely audible voice, he repeated, "It's nothing, nothing..."

His hands grew calm again, gently stroking

Catherine's body as if he were rocking a child to sleep or soothing an invalid.

When Catherine was in bed with the sheets drawn up under her chin, she began weeping aloud. Michel heard her sobbing through her tears, "I'm married to a man who doesn't love me . . ." His long body crashed down upon her, heavily, like a tree. He kept begging her pardon, kissing her face, her breasts.

Towards morning Catherine had become a woman. Michel collapsed at her side like a drowned man, repeating, "You are the very devil, Catherine, you are the very devil."

Catherine asked for the house keys on a little silver ring; she wanted to supervise the delivery of the groceries, the consumption of coffee, the washing, ironing and folding of the linen. She asked for coloured brooms and black soap.

Michel begged her not to go out on errands. He insisted that she stay quietly at home, like a pampered cat in the captive world of rain. He showed her all the treasures of the chests and cupboards that were not under lock and key.

He forbade her to look after the household accounts or to dismiss the servant as she had asked. He became increasingly taciturn, his golden gaze fixed like a burnt-out sun, and he doomed his wife to a similar dream.

Catherine liked to lock herself in the tiny bathroom with its mirrored walls. The warm water, perfumed soaps, the bathtub green as a leafy hollow, the creams and the perfumes were an endless delight. She spent hours lying under billows of soapsuds in the tepid water. She tried to hold her breath under water, as long as she could, thinking of fishermen diving for sponges and sightless fish.

Sometimes when Catherine found the isolation in which Michel had kept her since their wedding night particularly distressing, she would step out of the bath and wipe her feet with her own extravagantly perfumed hair twisted into a towel.

She tried on her dresses, one after another, parading slowly around the bathroom, greeted on all sides by her own erect grave reflection in the mirrors. She invented a ritual of discarding her skirts and petticoats in the twinkling of an eye, dropping a perfect circle of delicate fabrics at her feet. She then looped these great swaths around her arm like trophies before folding them all away in her perfumed cupboards.

But she longed to go to the market for vegetables, flowers and fruits. As soon as the servant had left, she would shout, cupping her hands around her mouth, biting off each word, imitating the rhythm and harsh intonation of the strawberry merchant who passed under her windows in June.

"Strawberries, strawberries, beautiful strawberries!"

She marched around the apartment trumpeting away as if calling the world to awaken from its sleep in the winter, in the rain. Then she threw herself into an armchair. Burying her head in the cushions, she grinned happily as if huge, wild hands had smeared her face with the odour and taste of strawberries.

"Catherine, Catherine," Michel said sadly, "what a whimsical little girl I've married."

And, like a weary embroiderer struggling to re-create the elusive design of a rare flower, he lowered his eyes to the patterns on the carpet. Catherine followed his glance. She explored with him the intricate forest of lines and colours as if she could, by sheer concentration, grasp the features of Michel's anguish, lost among the motifs of the carpet. Michel did not lift his head. Catherine grew weary of this game. In a moment of unbelievable emptiness, the designs of the carpet exploded before her eyes.

Hurriedly, she cried out, breathless, "How quiet it is here! Say something, Michel, please, speak, do something! I just know it, the clock's ticking will engulf the whole apartment!"

"Like a monstrous heart, Catherine, like the enormous heart of this tiny, quiet place where I've brought you."

He had not moved and spoke in the slow, even tone of someone reading aloud.

Catherine whispered, "Michel, you are evil."

Michel leapt to his feet.

"It's you who are evil, Catherine, a filthy woman, that's what you are, like Lia, like all the others!"

Catherine protested gently, almost tenderly.

"Michel, my husband, it's you who are evil."

An intolerable silence hung between them. Catherine stood before her husband with her fists tightly clenched, her gaze unfaltering, without tears, without reproaches, without the slightest sign of surrender, a thin, erect, severe girl rejected at her own threshold.

Michel and Catherine lived for a long time in these two single, wood-panelled rooms where the furniture was antique, the knickknacks unusual and everyday objects useless or broken. Between the two rooms ran a narrow, gloomy, bare corridor leading to the bathroom.

The hubbub of the city, with its marketplaces resonant with odours, its humid days, bumpy pavements, wide bustling squares, its pewter landscapes around the river and bridges, its loud, clamouring human voices, ebbed away like a wave under the high, closed windows.

Behind the curtains in this retreat, the colour of

a burnt cigar, with its carved mouldings and the aroma of books and nuts, Michel and Catherine avoided each other, kept bumping into one another, pretended to ignore each other. Living together in such cramped quarters, they were afraid of growing to hate one another.

All day long, Catherine sat in her high-backed chair, reading, embroidering, and sewing.

One day she pricked her finger on purpose and screamed out as if she'd been stabbed. Michel ran to her, alarmed by the shrillness of her scream. He sucked the blood dripping from her wounded finger. Falling to his knees, he encircled her legs with his arms and buried his head in the pleats of her dress, breathing the warmth of her lap. Without raising his head, he spoke, his voice hoarse against Catherine's stomach, as if calling from the depths of the earth, "Catherine, are you there? Are you there, Catherine?"

"Yes, I'm here, Michel."

Her thimble rattled along the floor, an interminable clatter.

"Please don't leave me, Catherine."

"I'm your wife, Michel, as you very well know."

"Catherine, it's terrible, I don't love you."

"I know, Michel, I know."

Catherine's voice, heartbroken, sang out its solitary little song.

"Don't abandon me, Catherine."

"I'm right by you, Michel, so close that I hear you breathing in my stomach like a baby inside me."

"I can only hurt you, Catherine, and yet I want you."

He leapt up abruptly, took two steps towards the door and said curtly, "Sit up, Catherine. Rest your head on the back of the chair, let your hair fall onto your shoulders. I don't want you to cry or laugh. Ah! How well you sew and embroider! What capable hands you have!"

Catherine looked at her hands, fervently, respectfully. "Michel, please let me do something else!" she pleaded. "The shopping, the meals . . . yes, that's it! I would love to bake a huge cake for Twelfth Night!"

"You're confusing things, Catherine. What is this nonsense about cakes? I haven't married a cook, have I? Your face flushed from the oven, your hair smelling of bread? I want to paint you in monochrome, all white and scentless, pale and cool like snow, still like water in a glass."

But Michel did not paint Catherine or anything else.

It was about this time that the piano – the dry, monotonous scales playing on throughout the night – began to disturb Catherine's sleep.

But all day she worked hard at becoming what Michel wanted her to be. She learned fables and poems by heart. These kept her amused during the long, silent hours spent at her needlework and sometimes these fables and poems, possessing a life of their own, burst like coloured veins in the middle of the whitest embroideries.

At other times, her needle kept picking out threads of rediscovered childhood and working them back again with quick, steady stitches in an attempt to ward off the stillness of the day.

At night she braided her hair carefully before going to bed. In the morning, after loosening her plaits, she studied herself in the mirror, looking for some resemblance between herself and the portrait of an infanta, the pure-blooded daughter of kings, so eagerly desired by Michel.

But in the shadows of dawn, instead of infantas, she kept encountering three clear, lifelike sisters with combs and flowing hair, circling around the lamp and smelling of coffee and toasted bread. The youngest one wept whenever anyone approached to comb her hair. The oldest had dark curls and the long shadow of her father fell across her.

The servant had tidied up everything and aired the room. She was an old woman, haughty, her eyes blue, huge and lashless.

The odour of Michel's late sleep had been swept away with the dust and ashes. Fresh sheets had been put on the beds and city air washed in through the wide-open windows like waves of sea water. From the bathroom Michel shouted that they wanted him to die from the cold. Catherine asked the servant to close the windows. But the servant, who had served Lia, scorned Catherine and would never obey her.

This woman, with her angular body, her insect eyes and her big, tobacco-coloured hands, would straighten out Michel's mess. Each afternoon, with a few brisk and precise motions, she set in order all the objects, pieces of furniture and scattered knick-knacks that were thrown drunkenly behind him.

Shen then pushed the high-backed, carved chair against the wall, saying, in the distant voice of someone addressing an absent deity, "Does Madame care to sit down?"

Ceremoniously, she handed Catherine a basket with books, linen, spools and scissors. Catherine took her seat, replaced by the servant like all the objects in this apartment that had been lost or carelessly picked up. Set like a bas-relief against the woodwork, she read or sewed until it was time for the evening meal, which she would eat facing Michel while he sat in silence, after the servant departed.

It was difficult to plan and prepare the meals, since Michel was irritated by any smell of cooking.

When, after a long succession of days and nights, Michel raised his head, his owl eyes fastened upon Catherine with surprise.

"Catherine, my little Catherine, what's happening? How lovely you are, how touching."

"It's a slow death, Michel, nothing but a very slow death."

Catherine's words both surprised and charmed Michel. He stammered, "What atrocious things you've learned to say, Catherine."

Catherine stood by the window, her nose pressed against the pane, the muslin curtain at her back, stubbornly staring at that bare, grey wall behind

which the world spun out its vehement, tumultuous
life.

"Why don't we ever go out, Michel? All those
concerts you promised me . . ."

Michel's face darkened. He seemed to be seeking
something particular and cruel in the blue spirals
of smoke from his cigarette. Then, in a low voice, he
said very distinctly, "That's so, Catherine, not a
single concert . . . And the season is drawing to a
close . . . not a single concert. It's nothing really,
Catherine, just the desire that's missing."

Catherine turned around sharply. The curtain
rippled over her in a lively froth of silvery light.
Michel, dazzled, put his hands over his eyes. He
begged Catherine not to stand there and to draw
the curtains against the sun. Catherine didn't budge,
her eyes open wide, haloed with light from head to
foot.

Michel believed that Catherine had nothing better to do in the enormous void where she was drifting than to surrender to the dream that had captivated her since childhood. He began his story:

"I'll reclaim the house and garden the whole summer and fall. I'll chase away Lia and that man. We'll cross the threshold together with your hand on my arm, like the true lords and masters of the place."

Catherine didn't know whether to believe Michel's words but his voice was so enticing and enraptured that she listened, her elbows on her knees, her chin cupped between her hands.

"Will we really go there together, Michel? And I'll be able to gather all the flowers in the garden I want?"

"We will hold sway over all the flowers, Catherine, even the sensitive camomiles that still quiver after they're picked."

Catherine mused in silence over the mystery of plants and all the vulnerable things of this world. Michel was speaking slowly, without looking at her, his eyes staring into the distance as if he were seeing it all that very moment.

"The piano reverberates there like a storm. Neither the house nor the garden at night can be strangers to the beautiful melody that rises from the merest touch of my fingers . . ."

"And me, Michel, what do I do in your house?"

"You Catherine? You listen to my music and enjoy it, you make it ring out more powerfully because your little life is so entwined with my house and garden that it quickens the tempo of my heart."

At that moment, Catherine started to speak, the whole burden of her life in her words.

"Am I fine enough, Michel? Fair and delicate enough? Have I grown pale enough and have I languished long enough in these two wood-panelled rooms? Have I read the most beautiful poems and learned by heart the most ironic fables? Am I not your wife and don't I have the right to be respected by the servant?"

"You are fine, Catherine, and fair and delicate. You shall enter the seigniorial manor by the front gate and the servant will bow down to you."

Catherine's voice broke. "Michel, what shall I do in the hot summer sun?"

"You must avoid the sun, Catherine, which discolours and burns. I'll teach you night games of fever and anguish."

He was growing animated, elated, drunk with words, believing that the end of his solitude was imminent. He ordered Catherine, right then and there, to don her finest evening dress, the colour of camellias, with gold strands set lightly in the soft fabric like mist.

When Catherine appeared, proud, innocent, and elegant, Michel insisted on circling her eyes himself with a precise black line.

"Catherine, how strange, you look like an idol now, with your blue eyes set in black like precious stones."

Knocking over the straw screen, as if hewing down a hedge, he made Catherine sit by the piano and began playing with abandon. Catherine remained there for a part of the night, attuned to Michel's presence singing within her. Sleep slowly overcame her as she curled up cozily in the armchair, her hair all tumbling down, her feet and hands tucked under the folds of her magnificent skirts.

Suddenly she was startled by the fury of a dissonant chord. She opened her eyes and saw Michel leave the piano, come towards her and lean over her. She felt his long hands smooth the hair from her face, sweeping the strands like a bunch of obtruding leaves into a knot on top of her head.

He scrutinized her with fierce attention, his tense features hardening with concentration. He smelled of liquor and sweat. He held Catherine's head gently by her long hair. He spoke to her in the third person, reproachfully, fascinated. "She's so beautiful, this woman, that I'd like to drown her."

The next day there was a knock at the door. Catherine opened it, recognizing Lia immediately, in spite of the darkness of the stairway.

There was a moment's silence. The smell of the apartment filled the entire space like an eager family pet noisily demanding attention. Lia took a deep breath, then crossed the threshold.

"I forgot my key and I didn't want to ring the bell and wake Michel up."

Disconcerted, Catherine stepped aside to let Lia enter. She was wearing very high heels which rang out clearly, sharply. She went into the kitchen and asked for a cup of coffee. Catherine prepared the coffee and served it to Lia in Michel's own delicate cup, while Lia's piercing gaze lingered over her every move. Lia remained standing, drank her coffee and then lit a cigarette with a flourish reminiscent of Michel.

"So you're Catherine..."

The low, husky voice sounded surprised, disdainful.

"Yes, I'm Catherine, and you, you're Lia ..."

"I shall be Lia forever, just as you'll be Catherine for as long as you can. Doesn't it seem strange to you not to be anything but yourself until your last breath, and ever afterwards, so they say?"

"Yes," said Catherine, turning the tap full force over Lia's cup, "but I never thought about it."

She swung around to face Lia.

"But then, what does it matter that I'm Catherine, that I can't change it? I'm Michel's wife and that's just fine."

Lia blew a puff of smoke at the ceiling.

"Really, you're Michel's wife and you believe that?"

Catherine stared blankly at Lia's profile, at that long, very black, narrow eye, that aquiline nose, that small, firm bottom perched high on long thin legs, that noble, bizarre look of a sacred bird.

"When does the servant arrive?" Lia continued.

Catherine didn't answer and wanted only to leave the room. Lia, having just settled herself in the armchair, drawled in a deceptively gentle tone, "But what are you doing? Michel mustn't be wakened; the daylight irritates him, pains him. The less he has of it, the happier he is. Surely you're aware of that?"

Taken aback, Catherine sat down on the stool she used for peeling vegetables.

Lia talked about the pain that light had inflicted on Michel from the most sensitive years of his childhood. The servant used to take them both, wearing large straw hats, to pick strawberries in the fiery heat of July. Even then Michel complained in the whining voice of a sickly child about the cicada's shrill song and the burning summer sun. He wanted to stay in the cool shade of the house till evening.

Sorrowfully, Catherine recognized that Lia's words held the same charm as Michel's. She spoke in a whisper, deeply conscious of the awkwardness, the urgency, and the truth of her own words. "I've always loved the daylight and the summertime . . ."

"You seem rather pale for a girl who likes the sunshine. But I see my brother dresses you well . . ."

There was a lengthy silence. The women became acutely aware of the objects and furniture in the kitchen. It was as if each had hurled them in turn at the other's head. Catherine's arrangement struck at Lia and she mentally restored everything to its original disorder, while Catherine's eyes followed Lia's, tidying it up again.

Then Lia started smoking again, unable to drag her eyes away from this silent, small girl hunched on a stool, facing her. When it was almost time for the servant to arrive, Catherine could no longer sit still. She jumped up and said to Lia, "You're out of cigarettes. I'll go get you some . . ."

She hurried off to ask the servant not to come that day, for she was afraid of being humiliated in her own home before the woman.

The suspicious surprise of the servant when Catherine told her not to come, then buying cigarettes at the corner cigar store, the storekeeper's grin, the big, blue sun over the porous city, then again the dim stairway and the stuffy wood-panelled rooms.

At the doorway she realized that Lia had wakened Michel and was speaking quietly to him. Catherine began to rinse the lettuce under the tap, then she decided to peel the carrots and leeks.

Brother and sister were arguing bitterly. Words and snatches of phrases flew about, winging through the door, piercing darts that were retracted immediately, chewed over, whispered syllable by syllable, confused, buzzing and plaintive. Each reproached the other of the same treason. Lia pointed out that Michel's marriage equalled her own misdeed.

Catherine let the water from the tap flow over her hands as if washing wounds. Not for a second did she stop scraping her vegetables.

She prepared the meal and set the table meticulously.

Michel and Lia appeared, still flushed with the explosion of their quarrel, furious and excited, identical siblings like two long, lean, self-sufficient thoroughbreds.

Didn't his sister even have that same peculiar mark formed by a tiny vein in the shape of a Y on Michel's forehead? Michel had once told Catherine that this was the sign of poets. And this sign was upon Lia like a tiny claw mark.

Catherine was afraid that Michel would reproach her for her flushed cheeks. He didn't notice anything, nor did he comment on the servant's absence. It was Lia who was surprised.

Catherine explained that in such a cramped apartment there was no room for another person; besides, she really preferred looking after her own household. She watched Michel carefully as she spoke. But nothing stirred in that faint, yellow light filtering through his wide, lowered lids. Catherine promised herself to dismiss the servant.

The summer was drawing to a close and there was no
mention of returning to the seigniorial manor.

Michel and Lia never spoke of it. This rather
surprised Catherine. There seemed to be a tacit
agreement between brother and sister about their
childhood home, condemned now to a summer solitude that scorched the trees and released brambles
and weeds in the garden.

The evening meal gathered Michel, Catherine
and Lia together around the table, to be served by
Catherine. Brother and sister gave themselves to a
witty exchange of words — light, elliptical conversations from which Catherine was excluded but

which inscribed themselves in her heart, shy sacred signs of the mystery of Michel.

Sometimes Lia's contained voice rose unexpectedly, arresting and sensual, and Michel's would answer, steady, pure, weary.

The summer night air was like a warm muzzle rubbing against the closed windows. With the shutters fastened, the apartment was cool and deep like a cellar. Defying the seasons, Michel and Lia seemed to want to create their own exclusive kind of weather, motionless and retrospective.

Their conversations had neither beginning nor end. They were resumed with passion each evening, without any apparent pretext, only to die away gradually or break off in the middle of a sentence or a word. Like fighting cocks, brother and sister confronted each other, face to face, having unknowingly reached the ill-guarded approaches of each other's furious hearts.

Lia threatened to leave. Michel begged her to stay. She shrugged her shoulders, impatiently. Then Michel screamed at her to get out immediately. The door slammed, Lia's heels clattered away in the resonant silence of the carpetless staircase.

A week passed and Lia had not returned to the apartment. Michel was very anxious. He blamed Catherine for Lia's absence.

Lia came back, silent and stiff, this tall, terracotta girl with her narrow, bony hips. There followed interminable speechless evenings amid cigarette smoke and the light tinkling of glasses.

Brother and sister busied themselves playing endless games of solitaire on the patterns of the carpet. The game seemed so sad and serious that Catherine thought that this was undoubtedly how deposed kings and queens whiled away away their time of exile. Catherine slowly worked at her needlepoint, sighing sleepily. She would drift off into fragmented dreams in which Michel and Lia appeared as the king and queen of hearts, crowning each other over and over, endlessly, through eternity.

Not once did Michel show any surprise at the new dishes Catherine contrived for him, leaning over him as if watching for the effects of a magic potion.

"Do you like it, Michel?"

Her hands bustled from the table to the oven, passing right under Michel's nose, a little cut darkening the root of her right thumb at the point where the palm swells up like the throat of a bird.

Silence enclosed Michel. Lia, too, was abstracted, oppressed, a stone urn powdered with sand, tilted for many years over the earth, absorbed by it.

Catherine's eyes darkened with concentration as she watched Lia being overcome by a kind of melancholy stupor that was slowly tainting her, drying her up like a lingering sunstroke.

To Catherine, life seemed increasingly strange. One day Lia refused to have any wine or meat or coffee or any seasonings. Catherine prepared a little rice for her; it was like an offering for the dead.

Lia had just broken off with her lover.

Soon Michel was complaining that the strong odours from the kitchen wearied him. He joined in Lia's fast and would no longer eat anything but the blandest food.

Catherine carefully noted down the names of the

herbs she had learnt from the servant. And sometimes, in the evening when time was dragging, she named them, one after the other like living companions. The names rose up, one at a time, breaking almost immediately on her tongue, dispersing their flavour intact: marjoram, basil, rosemary, bay leaf and sage.

"What are you singing there so seriously under your breath, Catherine, are you calling up the spirits?"

And Lia let her book fall on to her lap. Her beautiful strange eyes, like thin black stains of wet ink, paused for a second on Catherine.

"I'm not singing anything, I'm not singing anything, I'm bored."

Lia returned to her book. Michel was reading, too. It seemed like some austere study hall guarded by silence. Catherine began to think that with all this severity, brother and sister might well betray the little blue star engraved in the middle of their foreheads.

It was as if the world had lost all feeling until the day Lia suddenly stopped reading, buried her face in her hands, tears streaming through her thin fingers. Michel stood up. He looked at Lia, blankly, reproachfully. Catherine grew very pale. Then as Lia's sorrow showed no sign of abating, Catherine approached her, speaking to her as to a sick child.

"Lia, you mustn't cry, you're so beautiful, just like an Egyptian queen."

She softly placed her hands on Lia's face, pulled away the clenched fingers and kissed the hard, burning, salty cheek.

Lia was astonished. Then she pulled Catherine's small, fresh face fiercely towards her, murmuring in her ear that she was "sick with love".

Lia's unhappy passion distressed Catherine. It seemed to her that even the young woman's shadow became alive, lashing her heart. The whole apartment moved to the tumultuous rhythm of Lia's sorrow, Lia's anger, Lia's tears and the memories of Lia's seared flesh. And Michel faded into the background, bleaching before Catherine's eyes like someone who has never loved.

She would have liked to ask Lia about the delicate aspects of lost love. But she didn't dare and kept quiet, content to watch Lia, avidly scrutinizing her brown, dry, young body for traces of the fire, for the secret of one who has given herself and been taken.

When Lia, without a smile or a word, let down her long, black, shiny hair, then Catherine was especially happy and content. She would bring combs and hairpins and hold the mirror without moving during the whole lengthy hairdressing. Lia said, "Give me something to drink, Catherine."

Catherine brought her water in a clouded glass. Lia's lips were dry, as if she were feverish. After gulping down the water, she pressed the glass slowly against her cheek, her forehead.

"Ah! How good it is, how cool."

Then she shivered, "It's so cold here, Catherine."

Then Catherine bent over the fireplace and relit the fire. Soon Lia was holding her hands over the flames to warm herself and also, she said, to see her skeleton in "the flaming transparence of her fingers".

Catherine began to embroider linen with Lia's monogramme. She loved the leathery smell of Lia's luggage so brightly splashed with the names of the foreign lands she had visited with her lover. Lia gave Catherine two crude pearls to make into earrings.

One evening when it was raining heavily, Catherine begged Lia not to return to her hotel. She invited her to spend the night on the grey sofa in the kitchen and brought her a woollen blanket and two sheets. The next morning, Catherine, awakening early, had to stay in bed a long time, not daring to move for fear of disturbing the sleeping brother and sister.

Michel kept out of the way. With a gloomy eye, he observed the comings and goings of Catherine and Lia. Burying in his heart his anxiety at this friendship between the two women, he was careful not to intervene and take Lia away from Catherine.

Sometimes Lia asked Catherine to read to her. Catherine read badly, in a monotonous voice, stumbling over difficult words, occasionally lifting her eyes from her book to catch, were it only momentarily, a kind of ecstatic death that swept from time to time across Lia's face, smoothing her eyelids, pinching her nostrils, stiffening all her features.

Catherine wondered what sovereign power this was that seized Lia in the midst of such barren evenings and quietly, right under the eyes of Catherine and Michel, transported her to the other side of the world.

One evening Catherine called to Lia, fearful of

losing her in the bottom of an abyss and, along with her, the secret of that deep enchantment. Lia blinked her eyelashes and colour slowly flowed back into her cheeks. She stretched and very wearily asked Catherine, "You little fool, why are you bothering me? I know how badly you read. I've not been blind to any of your faults, you can be sure of that, but I was so far away and so happy that nothing could hurt me."

She tried to take the book out of Catherine's hands, but Catherine held her arm.

"Lia, please answer me, you're thinking of him, aren't you? It's *he* who all of a sudden makes your face turn pale, as if he were dragging you to the end of the world?"

"To the very doors of death, Catherine. If I were to tell you that, you wouldn't understand. But aren't you rather forward this evening?"

She seemed to swell up with anger. She stared at Catherine, who, without lowering her eyes, persisted, repeating in a clear voice, "Lia, even if you're angry, answer me. I want to know so badly. Why did you break off with this man you love?"

"How dare you ask me such a question? Never mind. I'm afraid my answer won't satisfy you at all; we're not of the same world, you and I. Listen carefully. I left him, freely, because of my pride, for an offence he committed against me without knowing it, and neither his heart nor his body had anything to do with it."

"I don't understand. I don't understand," Catherine repeated in despair.

"Remember the tale of 'The Princess and the Pea'," said Michel, who had drawn near. His face was beaming. He leaned towards Lia, offered her his arm and slowly, as if for a dance, led her to the piano.

Lia began playing, calmly, confident of her skill.
Michel was pained by a perfection he could never
attain, yet at the same time soothed. It was as if Lia
had freed him from an effort beyond his strength.
She was playing in his stead.

She also started painting, after scraping clean the
palette Michel had covered with Catherine's colours. Lia tried again and again to capture the ochre
red of the land of the *seigneurs*, as it melded with the
black heart of the pines. But she never finished her
great chaotic, coal-black and blood-red canvasses.

Lia's canvasses so tormented Michel that he begged her not to paint any more. Lia looked him straight in the eye and immediately announced that she would give a concert soon. At this news, Michel felt a bitterness so great in the depths of his being that his face seemed to age on the spot.

The closer the date of the concert came, the more Michel complained of the fever that attacked him at night, chilling and burning him at the same time. Lia spoke of nothing but pianos, concert halls, acoustics and critics. Then she sat down at the piano and practised till morning.

Michel listened to his sister, searching for faults, pursuing them, anticipating them, creating them, all with the intense concentration of someone entreating a destructive god. Up to the last moment he hoped Lia wouldn't give this concert. He was banking on the fact that she wouldn't be able to bridge that formidable gap that separates the best-laid plan from its complete realization in the light of day. That was the point where he himself always balked, like a rearing horse.

The evening of the concert, several minutes before her departure, Lia stood composing herself, pressing her hands flat against her skirt. Michel reproached her sharply for destroying the palette of seashore colours that he had prepared for Catherine's portrait.

Lia restrained herself from leaping at him, and turned slowly around, subduing her rage with a sinuous movement of her long neck. She was in perfect control of her still impassive face, of the hard, heavy burden of her heart, but her hands started trembling.

"My poor Michel, it's really pointless to work yourself up into such a state. You'll redo your palette when you can and, as for Catherine, you'll invent her all over again, as pale, sweet, transparent and empty as you want; you have a whole lifetime for that. But I'm going to play right now, and I beg you not to make me more nervous . . ."

Michel had drawn close to her. He was breathing noisily, anger emanating from his entire body. He spoke through his teeth, cracking each word like a nut.

"You won't play at this concert, will you, Lia? Please. See how your hands tremble . . . You know very well you'll never be able to do it . . . Look, just look, your hands are trembling . . . You feel them trembling, don't you? . . . Lia, your hands are trembling . . ."

Lia took a step back, then sprang forward and slapped Michel twice with all her might. Her long, brown hands grew calm again. Gently and with great care, she drew on her doeskin gloves and left.

Michel bathed his burning cheeks in cool water, then lit up a cigarette, which he immediately extinguished.

Startled by this extraordinary scene, Catherine did not dare move. Suddenly, Michel's voice sounded at her ear, hoarse, rude. He must have called her several times already and was growing impatient.

"Catherine, I'm speaking to you, do you hear, Catherine, my wife?"

Catherine could not move or speak. Again she heard the sound of the slaps whistling through the air, exploding in her head. She cried out and put her hands to her face.

Michel stood before her. He dragged her to the bed and took her awkwardly, furiously.

Lia did not come back the next day or the following days. Michel pretended not to notice. All his efforts in the tiny apartment were devoted to fleeing Catherine: Catherine's eyes, the rustle of her dress, the sound of her step, the swish of the comb in her hair, even the murmur of her sleep. He would have liked to drive his shame out as one throws a girl on to the streets. Catherine was the source of his shame and, through a thousand subterfuges, he avoided being in the same room with her.

He pored over the newspapers and musical journals, feverishly searching for an article about Lia's concert. Occasionally, there was a reference to a tall dark girl with bronzed hands who had learned her piano lessons thoroughly, and played well, correctly, even flawlessly, but without inspiration.

When Michel was certain that there was no mention anywhere of "genius", of "sacred communication", of "inspired medium", his joy was boundless and he wanted to be reunited with Lia.

One winter evening she returned. She was very weary. When she had taken off her coat, Michel and Catherine saw that she was still wearing the black concert dress that fitted her thin body like the sheath of a sword.

It was Michel who played for Lia now with a kind of lighthearted peace. Lia folded her hands, leaned her head on his shoulder, and seemed to cover herself in ashes.

She no longer wore any rings or bracelets, she seemed to have forgotten about her lilac dress and the other saffron-coloured one that fitted tightly over her hips like bandages covered with black scribblings. She continued to wear her concert dress, which grew shiny and wrinkled. One Sunday, she added a little linen collar, which she asked Catherine to iron.

Lia made herself completely at home in the apartment. Just before dawn, she would stub out her cigarette, stretch out on the sofa in the kitchen and sleep, immobile, until late in the afternoon.

After dinner, Michel played slow, serene pieces for Lia. Lia, like a desiccated raven, did not seem to hear anything. Michel spoke animatedly about the purity of rediscovered childhood. Growing impatient, Lia begged him to be quiet. If, occasionally, Michel addressed Catherine, it was only to praise Lia's thinness, which he compared to the pure lines of the spirit. One evening, Catherine heard him saying to Lia, "Lia, you are as transparent as water, my sister, water, that is you, Lia."

One more time, Michel's embittered body, fired up with a brief glimmer of pleasure, fell upon Catherine, only to complain afterwards, like a wave that destroys as it ebbs, that love was corrupt.

Order seemed to prevail. The roles had been cast, once and for all, clearly and distinctly between Catherine and Lia. "Martha and Mary," thought Lia. "The innocent one cleans the house, her humiliated body ignorant of love. Michel's shame is upon her. And I, Lia, am the honour and the higher life of Michel. The world of our childhood, of endless leisure and wild anguish belongs to us alone."

But Lia was wasting away, sealing off her life, and her lips grew thin like those of very old women.

One day, there was talk of a visit from the notary. Michel was surprised and Lia seemed to go berserk. She urged Catherine to help look for her jewels, which were scattered about the apartment. When she had found them, she threw them in a handkerchief and folded the four corners together. The jewels clattered together like marbles.

Catherine looked forward eagerly to the notary's visit. Wasn't he the first visitor since her marriage?

The notary didn't come. It was Lia who spoke to Michel.

She dropped her jewels on the table with an

abrupt movement and told Michel she was giving them to him.

Michel recognized his mother's jewels. He recalled the trouble between him and his sister over these jewels. Without looking at her, he murmured, "What are you doing?"

"Take them, Michel. They're yours."

"It wasn't really worth it to have argued so bitterly with me about them the day our mother died."

Lia backed towards the door. She spoke curtly as if nothing she said could reach him.

"Michel, remember the illuminated Book of Hours that mother loved so much and that couldn't be found after death? Well, it was I who had hidden it. But I'm giving it back, I'm giving it to you, along with the rings and the emerald bracelet. Take it all, Michel, and the silver cross from Italy . . ."

"Lia, what's going on? I don't understand."

Lia raised her arms like someone hastily throwing things away before hurrying off.

"Take everything, Michel, everything, the piano, the rare books. I'm going to hurt you, Michel. But you understand, once two people have begun to hurt each other, sooner or later they reach the limit of the pain they can cause. It's inevitable, it happens, it has happened, it's horrible, and then it's over."

Again she lifted her arms. She was trembling, a great Fury crucified against the door.

"You can take it all, Michel, father's gun, the red boots he gave me for my tenth birthday, all the walking-sticks, the hunting crops . . ."

"Lia, what's happening? You're drunk, this can't be. Why are you stripping yourself in this way? I don't want your gifts. There is only one thing that's still close to my heart, the estate I own jointly with you, our shared childhood, so bitter and yet sweet."

Lia spoke quickly, leaning against the door.

"It's over, Michel, there isn't anything left, no more childhood, house, garden, park, they've all been taken, even the stagnant pond . . ."

Her tall body collapsed like a parched, broken reed. She rubbed her face with her bony, trembling hands. Michel seized her hands violently.

"Lia, what are you saying? Are you going mad?"

Angrily, Lia jerked herself away.

"No, not mad, lucid, clearsighted, hard."

"Tell me everything. What's happened?"

Lia cried, "The house is going to be sold!"

Michel's voice dwindled like a thread about to break.

"It's that man who's done this?"

Lia drew herself up, speaking with dignity, as if relating a dramatic story in which she had no part.

"I was subjugated to him until my final humiliation. Do you hear me, Michel, subjugated like a whipped bitch and I begged him on my knees to keep me and take me one more night, just one more night."

Michel turned away. "That filthy man. Lia, no, it's not true."

99

There was a moment choked with silence, broken only by Lia's breath rasping in her chest like an invalid's.

Michel raised his hands towards her in the vacant gesture of a distraught hypnotist.

"Wake up, Lia, you're dreaming, it isn't possible. How could this be?"

"Don't you remember the terms? The notary will explain them to you. That if one of us wants to sell the estate that's all that's required."

"But you can't want that, not you, Lia?"

Lia burst out laughing.

"I, Michel, want or not want? You know very well I no longer have a choice. There is a man who possesses me to the very marrow of my bones. I can only do what he wants. And what he wants, he wants very badly, I assure you. He had only to touch me and I yielded everything to him in one dizzy moment. Right from our first meeting, he coveted the house and garden. And right from the first touch of his fingers digging into my shoulder, I surrendered them to him."

She had collapsed on the carpet by the fireplace, her hair dishevelled, her head on her knees. With his hand, Michel pushed aside the jewels on the table. A ring rolled onto the ground. Lia was sobbing and calling to Michel, "Michel, Michel, please forgive me."

Michel did not move, groping for contemptuous words. The words hissed weakly through his teeth. "You, so proud, so noble . . ."

"I'll tell you everything, Michel, everything. The man has gone. He abandoned me like a loaf of old black bread that one throws away after breaking into. He sailed away on a worm-eaten boat. With every departure the flag is changed and the name of a different woman is painted on the hull. Once that boat was called 'Lia', the man was mine and I was his, the two of us entwined together like two vines."

"Shut up, Lia, shut up. Please!"

"I'm so cold, Michel!"

Michel pushed her aside. He bent over the hearth. The odour of dead ashes clung to his tear-dampened face. He lit a pathetic little fire, then got up and laid his hand upon his sister's shoulder. She raised her ravaged face to his.

"You know, Michel, your wish was granted the evening of the concert, because you had truly wished me that fear, from the bottom of your heart. I played badly because of that fear paralyzing each one of my fingers..."

"Forgive me, Lia, please forgive me."

He kissed her hair gently, as if afraid of hurting it. Lia lifted her head in defiance, breathing heavily, like a trapped animal.

"And your little girl you brought from the smelting town? You keep washing and polishing her like a fresh-water pebble. But what of her pale heart, what can you do about that? Soon you'll resemble your wan little girl; you'll tell me that the weather's fine and that love is calm and limpid like a lake of ice."

"Be quiet, Lia, you mustn't talk about Catherine."

"I will talk about Catherine! It's only fair that our childhood home should be taken from us. Didn't we betray it, both of us?"

"It's you who began, Lia ..."

The fire was drawing poorly and filling the room with smoke. Lia closed her eyes, speaking in a low, grumbling voice like a tired storyteller, dreamily scolding her children.

"Oh! how badly this fire draws! The mother has been gone now for five months. The father hunts all day, the servant has fled away and the two children, alone, crouching by the wood fire in the abandoned house make a pact swearing fidelity to each other!"

Michel had knelt at Lia's feet.

"Lia, Lia, how far away everything seems, how ruined, how soiled. What are we going to do now?

"Nothing, nothing, Michel, we are nothing, absolutely nothing, just two poor lost children. Oh! this smoke burns my eyes. My poor Michel, we're powerless; look, you don't even know how to start a fire."

Catherine came in, saw the brother and sister weeping, clinging to one another. Crossing the room, she lit the fire and prepared the coffee. Her hands were trembling. She concentrated on not dropping, upsetting or breaking anything, as if the very safety of her life depended on the steadiness of each of her movements. She stared for a long time at the tiny trail of steam escaping from the coffee pot. Perhaps for the first time, she felt a great rage submerge her sorrow, wildly seeking some outlet in her childish, subjugated being.

That night she dreamt. "The seigniorial manor was cursed and condemned to flames. The tall building blazed to the sky, then collapsed with a loud boom. A glowing splinter burned on Catherine's wrist for awhile, then disappeared completely as she moved off down the road."

Time slipped imperceptibly by Catherine, Michel and Lia.

In that confined corner by the fireplace, alternately powdered by ashes and burned by spitting logs, the brother established a kind of baroque camping ground. Here he invited his sister. Glasses, books, cigarettes and ashtrays overflowing with butts accumulated on the carpet, staking out Michel and Lia's territory. They hardly ever moved and, twice a day, Catherine would bring them white fish and rice.

Autumn passed, and then, in the middle of winter, Catherine fell very ill.

First, her hands failed, refusing any contact with the things and people of that household. She no longer interfered with the brother and sister's litter. Soon, the apartment resembled a chaotic bazaar. There was no one to go shopping and carry provisions back to the wood-panelled rooms. The brother and sister grew hungry. Lia nagged Catherine, who did not budge.

The servant had to be asked to look after the shopping and cooking again. She went about it all wrong, grumbling constantly. She was aging and wanted nothing more than to rest, giving free rein to the lamentations of a woman born into servitude.

Folding her idle hands, Catherine soon found the stuffiness of the apartment unbearable. She threw the windows wide open. Michel and Lia were horrified because it was very cold. But Catherine would not listen. She was smothering like someone on the verge of death.

Brother and sister wrapped themselves up in shawls and blankets. Lia declared that she couldn't live in a public square, exposed to every wind that blew. Angrily, she slammed the windows shut. Catherine immediately opened them again. She leaned out to catch in passing some scent of the earth that wasn't cursed.

All night long, offensive smells kept Catherine awake; old half-extinguished butts, dried-out woodwork, paints and turpentine (for Lia had begun to paint again), boiled fish, stale beer.

But by morning, one odour in particular irritated her; the musky stench of brown flesh that has been smothered in wool beside a little fire that filled the room with smoke and soot.

Catherine sat up in her bed, crying out "that she was fair and white, that deep inside she smelled of fresh snow and that she wasn't part of this alien race of impotent and saffron-coloured gypsies."

No one heard her cry. It was just before dawn. The steady breathing of the brother and sister reverberated from one room to the other with almost a regular beat. Catherine covered her ears with her hands. Her heart was beating to the point of breaking. Her palms throbbed wildly against her temples, echoing the plaintive sound of Michel's sleep, while Lia's harsh voice hissed furiously in her ear.

Catherine didn't sleep. It seemed as if she would never be able to sleep again.

First Lia's breathing changed, it subsided, turning into sighs, then yawns. Catherine imagined she was slamming the door between herself and Lia's wakening. But in the state of agonized waiting that gripped her entire body, Catherine no longer seemed capable of any movement. She anticipated every sound. As Lia stepped to the floor, Catherine's ear was already exploding with the light sound. One never knew exactly when Lia put on her slippers. Her feet seemed to leave the bed shod in felt.

Michel's sister went into the little corridor, her long hair trailing down her back. Catherine would have liked to smear the bathroom mirrors with soot so they wouldn't reflect any thin, bronzed image that morning.

Feeling Catherine's eyes fixed upon her, Lia swung around, surprised.

"Not up yet?"

Catherine didn't answer and turned her face to the wall.

When Lia came back, her hair fastened on top of her head, Catherine shut her eyes, the silhouette of her surprised and irritated sister-in-law still clearly visible on her lowered eyelids. Seconds later, she sensed each of Lia's movements as she slipped on her lingerie, pulled up and fastened her stockings and drew her faded dress on like a glove.

Catherine then counted the click-clack of the approaching high heels so accurately that she opened her eyes exactly when Lia pressed her face to the pages of an old psalter and began to sniff it hungrily like a bouquet of leather and ink. Conscious of Catherine's eyes on her, Lia spun around quickly, like a child caught in the act. She muttered through her teeth, "Aren't you asleep?", and left the room, slamming the door so sharply that behind the screen Michel started in his sleep.

Catherine was suddenly afraid of being shut in with Michel's inert body. The darkness seemed intolerable. She got out of bed, barefoot, each step an effort. "How everything here tortures me," she thought as the stench of Lia's first cigarette came wafting in under the door.

She opened two windows, one onto the courtyard and one onto the street, and paced nervously from one to the other, like a trapped animal seeking an escape. She was trembling with cold, continually comparing the courtyard and the street in a grave and mysterious game, as if her whole life suddenly hung on some elusive balance.

The curtains flapped in the breeze, and Michel snuggled down in his bed. With a drowsy movement he pulled the blankets over his shoulders, exposing his delicate feet. Catherine turned away.

When the pale winter day had faded away, Catherine measured the increasing anguish of all her senses. She had spent this miserable day stretched out on her bed, suffering from sounds and smells, from all she saw, touched, tasted. The servant, finding her very ill, called her "Madame". Twice, the old grey hands remade the bed and turned the pillow.

Catherine let herself be held, lifted, laid down, her hair tumbling over her white nightgown, a thin, malleable girl. Momentarily her head rested upon the servant's ample chest and she longed to return to the comforting world of mothers and sleep. She begged the servant to watch the door so neither

Michel nor Lia would come in. The servant guarded Catherine's bedroom. Brother and sister argued with the servant because there was no fire in the other room.

Not one cool spot on the pillow, Catherine thought.

The servant returned and addressed Catherine with great deference, as if she were mistress of the hearth. Waiting no longer, Lia strode in, walked resolutely to the fireplace, knelt down and rummaged in the fire with much poking about of tongs and the poker. A log rolled onto the carpet with a shower of sparks.

Brother and sister returned to their stations before the fire like two figurines of blackened wood. Michel reminisced about those silent autumn evenings when two children's capes smoked above a blazing fire in the immense kitchen.

"Lia, isn't this extraordinary? What, in fact, is the present? Don't you at this very moment smell that irritating stench of singed homespun cloth? You've purposely burned your cloak, hoping to find in 'that devil of a bouquet' as you used to call it, the pungent, humid flavour of a long day's duck hunt in the fog and swamp..."

"Odd bouquet, it's just the rug I burned."

Not a movement disturbed Michel and Lia's immobility. The sound of their voices surfaced, calm and monotonous, even and expressionless. They didn't look at one another, but appeared to address the dead heart of the fire.

"Lia, remember the bursts of light flaming on the copper pots and the walls polished by that beautiful time-worn sheen as dark as your skin."

Twice, a little muscle twitched furiously in Lia's cheek, like a scratch on the smooth skin stretched tightly over her bones.

"You're annoying me! I have other vivid memories of that huge kitchen with its scorched wood, its magnificent fire, its heavy, shiny, ancient pots and pans. I recall quite other sheens, other pigments and I become warm and alive again. Please be quiet. Don't speak to me of that cursed house."

Michel bowed his head.

Lia quickly continued, "And your wife, what will we do with her?"

"Are you speaking of Catherine?" And Michel's voice faltered. "She's sleeping, I think."

Catherine was playing dead. All the troubles of the world were piercing her flesh, as if she had been rooted to the spot by a spell.

Soon the sheets scorched Catherine's skin, her nightgown was as heavy as lead, her hands and feet grew
numb from the terrible chill creeping under her
nails. In this frenzy that overwhelmed her whole
body, Catherine hoarded up her tears, like a last
possible death she must keep in reserve.

She couldn't bear any food. And when she refused
to drink, sealing her dry lips, the servant told
Michel to call a doctor. Catherine protested that
she wasn't ill, it was just that there were too many
things in this house that she couldn't bear. She
ordered the piano to be locked up and begged the
servant to throw the key out in the street.

The servant obeyed her in everything, captivated by this rebellion of Catherine's and delighted to perform such a rare service in her old age.

Catherine had Michel and Lia's paintings ripped from the wall. The servant was instructed to knock down the straw screen and sweep away all traces of ashes and fire.

Catherine threw off her sheets and her nightgown, twisted her hair on top of her head in a hard chignon like a nut so that not a wisp would trail through this place of misery. She closed her eyes and fell silent, summoning deafness like a balm, and her nostrils pinched, rejecting all odours.

Her nakedness worried the servant for it was very cold in the fireless room with the windows wide open. Catherine accepted the servant's coat, thrown over her, but soon the smell of the poor old woman became unbearable. She was suffocating. The servant hurried off to fetch a doctor, and in her panic, she forgot to close the bedroom door.

Catherine lay exposed in her passion as if she were lying in state. The light from the open door fell on her closed face. She knew that the children of the *seigneur* were there, close by, within reach of her hand, watching her, stupefied. Michel approached the bed weeping. He put the covers back over her and murmured in a scarcely intelligible voice: "Catherine, are you going to die, you're so ill today? How beautiful you are, you've never been so beautiful, Catherine."

Catherine lay thinking: "How my death pleases

you, Michel," and she longed for the comfort of death. Michel spoke of immediately making Catherine's death mask. In her weakness Catherine dreamt that she was eating ripe peaches, alone, in an immense orchard, where thick trees cast deep shadows like holes on the warm grass. Then, as the dream continued, she felt within herself, once again, the sound of Michel's adoration mounting, mounting like a wave about to submerge her. Soon her life would be ended. She struggled against the long, elegant, weightless hands caressing her face like sensitive leaves stirred by the breeze. A distant voice repeated wearily, summoning fleeing dark powers, "Don't move, don't move, stay still, there, there, see how she rests . . . Don't move . . . Don't move . . ."

She grew limp, languid, exhausted, without strength; she was about to dissolve into a flood of tears when the voice of her delirium soared again, clear and precise, rising from the bottom of her alerted heart: "This woman is so beautiful that I'd like to drown her."

She gave a piercing shriek, opened her eyes and saw the terrified face of Michel leaning over her. She pushed him away, hitting him squarely in the chest with both hands.

Michel drew back, startled by Catherine's violence. Lia watched him disdainfully.

Just then, the servant announced the doctor's arrival. Lia was wrapped in a beautiful cashmere shawl which no one had ever seen her wearing before. She whispered to her brother, barely moving her lips, "That child is possessed. If you let her continue, she'll destroy you. She has already had the piano locked up and your paintings torn from the wall. She can't bear any noise or colour connected with us. Beware of your little female with her five uncultivated, aggravated senses."

Drawn, as to a mirror, by Catherine's painful likeness to himself, Michel did not hear Lia's words. He drew near again, seeking in vain for a glance from his wife. Catherine had sworn not to open her eyes or respond to Michel's mute pleas. Michel was claiming the complicity with death on Catherine's burning face as his right and pleasure. Michel's lost love suddenly welled up anew in her heart. She was struggling for her life against the strange love of this man.

PART THREE

"... and a very tiny ring
for the dream."
JULES SUPERVIELLE

The servant parted the curtains, leaned out the window, and remarked that the weather was still fine.

Catherine looked through her lashes and saw her tanned hands against the white sheet. She plunged back into the darkness and for the first time could imagine the peppery colour of the geraniums without fear. She called to the servant and asked her how high the sun was.

The angular, aged servant moved slowly and jerkily. She went back to the window and, craning her neck and knitting her brows, answered "that the sun would soon rise and the whole roof of the terrace would be lit up and radiant with the colours Madame likes so much."

Catherine came to the window, wearing a transparent blue nightgown that shimmered over her slight body like a reflection on a river. She peered out and saw that the tiled roof was glistening, its salmon pink colour touched with watery light. She thought of juicy watermelons, which made her hungry and thirsty.

Complaining continually about the morning wind, the servant brought her breakfast. Catherine hardly listened to her. She was thinking of the geraniums she wanted but at the same time she was apprehensive of their violent scent.

"Do you think the scent of geraniums could harm me?"

"Only Madame can know that!"

Catherine wearily closed her eyes, thinking about smells that were pleasant and those that were repulsive. She murmured: "Ah! How strange all this is and how much my senses have suffered."

Not knowing how to shape her strong, massive face into an expression of solicitude, the servant drew closer to Catherine. She smoothed the pillows.

"Does Madame need anything?"

"Nothing, Aline, nothing, I assure you."

And it seemed infinitely sad not to have anything more to ask for on such a fine day.

The servant hesitated for a second, then brusquely fastened to her bodice a pin she had just picked up. She left, carrying the breakfast tray.

Catherine returned to the window and leaned upon the sill. Her eyes scanned the sea. She stayed there for a long time, studying the neighbouring house with its little hanging balcony where the geraniums' vermilion warmth stood out among the charcoal black bars. Someone had just watered the flowers; their aroma rose like incense to the sun.

The two houses were as close together as in a crowded city. And all around stretched the broad, solitary expanse planted with olive trees, sloping in terraces to the edge of the sea.

Towards evening the sea grew stormy. Light receded from the sky and earth, rising like mist from the lonely rage of the sea.

Catherine went for a long walk on the pier, whipped by a wind that snatched at her black cape and at the strands of her blonde and tousled hair. She paused for a moment on the terrace of a café. The tables were sticky with salt and the chairs were rusty. She was soon anxious to rejoin the procession of strollers in the wind, feeling inexplicably happy for it seemed to her that all fates were at the same time anonymous and simple and pathetic.

When she returned home, the lights were on in

the living room. The servant was waiting for her, grumbling. She reproached her for bringing sea breezes, potent as bundles of algae, back to the house which had already been thoroughly aired and closed up for the night.

"And after I carefully got rid of every one of the odours so Madame could sleep peacefully."

"I'll sleep, Aline, don't worry, don't fuss so much about shutting up the house, leave the window open so I can hear the waves better. I also want to see that wicker armchair and the yellow table in the garden next door."

The servant turned her back to Catherine, her voice regretful and haughty amid the din of clattering dishes.

"There are two chairs, Madame, and two people, an old lady and a young gentleman. They drank tea in the garden and ate cakes. They didn't seem to know each other."

Catherine lifted the curtain and leaned against the window.

"They've gone in now, Madame."

And Aline left the room, carrying Catherine's damp coat.

A window lit up on the second floor of the neighbouring house. Catherine dropped the curtain. She went to sit near the table, by the lamp, as attentive as if she were trying to touch the mystery of others in the night.

Often, in the evenings, as she lay in her huge, calm bed, Catherine was seized by a desire to be rocked. She detained the servant, using all sorts of pretexts – the sheet which was trailing on the left, the night light that shone bright as day, the cretonne curtain flapping against the the windowpane, the forgotten glass of water, the poorly fastened shutter. She loved to follow the comings and goings of this large woman as she celebrated rites around the bed with strong hands.

At one moment, the heavy-set, rigid form was passing in front of the open bay window, scattering the shadows of leaves shimmering on the floor tiles, the next she was approaching the bed. Catherine looked forward to that brief moment when, without any tender or visible magic, the servant, her chest studded with pins like a gleaming coat of mail, would bend her impassive face towards her and brusquely wish her good-night.

Thus it was that every night Catherine encountered the intangible and unwavering strict faith of the servant who had chosen her for mistress.

The first time this had happened was during Catherine's illness, a little after the doctor's visit.

Michel and Lia were discussing his recommendation that Catherine leave the narrow confines of her room as quickly as possible. He had spoken of deep depression, convalescence, a change of air, space and sun. Michel's tears, his livid pallor and his panicky movements all reminded Catherine of the unhappy child she had promised herself to comfort one day.

"You won't go away, Catherine? Please. We both suffer from the same wound. I don't want you to leave me. And where would you go, you're so fragile? Look, I beg you, look, see how alone and miserable I am."

Catherine was trembling. Her shaky will, straining towards a salvation that would demand all her efforts, might have faltered from one moment to the next. The servant stood by the bed, a statue of justice, weighing in her severe heart the strength of the man and women confronting each other before her eyes. She refrained from betting on one or the

other, hoping that the strongest would be irrevoc-
ably revealed to her.

Catherine spoke, her face turned to the wall.
Michel had to bend over the bed, straining to hear
the almost subterranean answer escaping from her
cramped chest. She murmured that she was suffering
terribly, that Michel's breath was burning her
cheek. Michel straightened up, his hands stretched
before him, a blind man groping for reality in an
empty world. Then Catherine said in a clear, slow
voice that she wanted nothing so much as to go far
away from him and never return.

The servant stepped forward and said that she
would accompany "Madame" wherever she wanted
to go. Lia swung around so sharply, her shawl slipped to the floor. The servant pretended not to notice
Lia's anger or Michel's tears. She sat Catherine up
in bed, helping her to rise.

Lia was speechless before the servant, so astonished was she by the sudden revelation of Catherine's height when she rose from her bed as if emerg-
ing from a shadowy adolescence.

In the spacious room where seaside breezes stirred
amid the furniture polished the colour of wood ants,
the servant had now finished her nightly rounds.

"Madame has no further need of me?"

She hesitated for a moment. Encumbered by her
weight, she turned on her heels and slowly left the
room.

Catherine extinguished the lamp. She waited several seconds until all the objects and furniture in this room of hers re-emerged from the shadows. With delight, she located the gleaming chest of drawers with its brass fittings and the little creamy carpet lying flat on the red tiles. She sometimes dreaded the fumbling return of the servant, who thought her mistress asleep and was worried about her exposure to the night air.

It was mid morning, and the roof of the terrace glistened with light. Catherine walked to the railing. She closed her eyes, momentarily dazzled by the sun, and the strong scent of flowers caught at her throat. She leaned towards the neighbour's garden. A young man was sitting in the hot sun, straight, motionless and stubborn, dedicated to a lengthy and voluntary baking in this ceramic oven. His back was turned to Catherine.

The servant passed by without stopping, a basket of freshly washed linen over her arm. She mumbled harshly: "That man looks dull and cloddish, a real peasant."

Catherine followed her into the courtyard and helped hang up the laundry. For a moment Aline was tempted to admire the young women's skilful movements but finally felt only contempt. "This girl knows how to work and is betraying her origins," she was thinking. And she added aloud, that "all masters went bad in the long run!"

Then suddenly she ran inside, abandoning her basket on the lawn.

Towards noon, Aline, who was preparing lunch, came to tell Catherine that there were four people eating in the neighbouring garden under the olive trees.

"Are you quite sure of what you're saying, Aline?"

Embarrassed by the servant, Catherine's voice suddenly cracked and rang false. She ate slowly, forcing herself to hide her delight at the thought of the neighbouring garden suddenly inhabited by unknown men and women. She grew impatient at moments, repelling the burning image of a strong head with thick, cropped hair and the powerful neck of a dumb stag that kept appearing before her eyes like the fiery spot when one has stared too long at the sun.

The next morning the servant counted five people in the garden. Catherine recognized the young man, a little apart from the others, mending a fishing net.

All day long, Catherine walked around barefoot, equally enjoying the rough and smooth patches, as if all the earth beneath her feet was pleasurable. She busied herself for a long time in the garden, under Aline's haughty eye.

"Madame plods around the flowerbeds barefoot and she's ruining her nails with this weeding!"

Catherine looked down at her hands and feet, which were matted with dirt. "Here I am, as black as my father at the end of a day's work!" she thought. And she prayed that she would once again be granted the grace of living humbly and gradually through the renewal of her patient body.

That evening she wrote to her youngest sister whom she hadn't seen since her marriage to Michel, describing at great length how they cared for the soil and plants in this region.

Since leaving the wood-panelled apartment, Catherine had very carefully, timidly, allowed the summer to colour her gently.

"Madame's turning as brown as bread," observed Aline.

And Catherine stood before the servant, as straight and tall as on the day of her separation from Michel. But the next moment she lost all her power over Aline's soul, incurring her contempt by a long visit to a peasant family in the mountains.

She had returned a little breathless, with some black bread and olives, and began talking about a little child she had held in her arms. Aline stiffened with anger, muttering through her teeth about the baseness of the poor and the horrid smell of their children that clings to you like the plague.

Catherine retorted with a sort of joyful fury that

this smell of poverty reminded her of her childhood. She added that once the holidays were over, as soon as she returned to the city, she would look for a job. She refused to eat the dinner Aline had prepared and munched her bread and olives, standing on the doorstep.

Then she went out for a long walk on the pier. Near the harbour, she met the young man returning with some fishermen. He stared at Catherine for a long time, intensely, without smiling.

The servant once again indicated the neighbouring garden.

"There are too many people there. All the shutters are open now. Chairs and umbrellas have been set out. Madame can't avoid all that. You'll have to go down to the sea in full view of everyone. It's a *pension*, Madame. Who would have believed it?"

Catherine went down to the sea. She felt uneasy, as if someone's eyes were following her.

Two lovers had taken over her favourite cove. From the top of a rock she watched them for a long time, finding them neither beautiful nor shapely in their bathing suits, surprised that love was bestowed so gratuitously. She bathed, dried herself in the sun, bathed again, tarried on the beach, staring at the sea, the rocks, the bathers, the flat horizon.

On her way home, she again met the young man by the harbour. At first she avoided his eyes. But his bare chest seemed to bar her way. She raised her head. A smile passed fleetingly over the man's face; perhaps he, too, was very serious. Or was it because Catherine was trembling that she saw only an indistinct wave suddenly blurring the clear features?

The servant was waiting for Catherine. She was surprised by her tardiness and remarked on the way the coolness of the night fell upon the day in a sudden downpour. She explained that summers in this region never fully arrived until the cicada's song rustled like a forest fire through the treetops.

"Who's told you all this, Aline? Your're not from this country and you hardly mingle with the folks around here?"

Aline replied that nothing escaped her and that, like a threatened, alert soldier, she was aware of everything around her. While she said this, she watched Catherine through her hard, shadowless eyes. As if leading silent beasts to water, she took the flowers out for the night.

Catherine picked up some mimosa balls that had tumbled onto the ground. Their colour still amazed her. Hadn't she always believed that mimosas were blue? And she thought uneasily of the servant, an old, worn woman with a gaze as sharp as hailstones. And she promised herself that she wouldn't lie, even if her face completely revealed her shameless joy.

The cicadas rent the air with their rasping song and the fire of noon settled over the land.

Catherine and the young man now met every day on the beach, though they never exchanged a word. Marked by the same sign – oil, sun, water and salt – they would camp quite close to each other, not missing any of the other's comings and goings, linked together in the wind like silent sailors.

Catherine liked to watch the youth swimming in the open sea and, when he stepped onto the pebbles, she looked forward to the moment when he would pass near her. A boyish smile then revealed his strong teeth and momentarily lit up his face with its snub features.

One morning when Catherine had arrived at the beach earlier than usual, hoping to avoid the heat of day, he approached her, greeted her awkwardly, introduced himself as Bruno and began to talk about his holidays, which were drawing to a close, about deep-sea fishing, and excursions to the mountains.

Catherine was vexed that he had addressed her as "Madame". The flat sound of his constrained voice irritated her. She observed his earnest features now so close to her with ill-humour. For an instant, she felt that all complicity between this stranger and herself was suddenly fading away like a long dream. She spoke confusedly about the sun, risk of headaches and the pitiless heat of the sky.

"Excuse me, Madame, but I'd like to say good-bye to you. I'm leaving tomorrow."

Catherine's pale eyes widened in her sunburnt face. In a sort of stupor, she stared at this man who was going to leave. Desire was stirring within her, awakened, threatened, surpassing the tranquility of dreams. She stammered: "You must never say good-bye, Monsieur, that brings bad luck. We will undoubtedly see each other again, since you're not leaving till tomorrow."

She held out her hand to the young man, who squeezed it abruptly. He strode off towards the town. For a moment afterwards, Catherine felt on her palm the pressure of a small callus on the fourth finger of the young man's right hand. Then, glancing towards the pier, she noticed the servant hurrying away.

That afternoon Catherine did not go to the beach. She settled down in the cloth lounge chair under the olive trees on the side opposite the neighbouring villa. She stretched out her legs and closed her eyes, feigning calmness, while her heart was beating as if about to break in her chest, throat and wrists. She feared Aline's gaze and at the same time would have liked to seek refuge near this old woman who had been Michel's servant.

"What a lovely dress! Is Madame expecting a visitor?"

The servant had approached without a sound and spoke through compressed lips, holding a long thread between her teeth. Catherine spoke with an effort, "Do you want me to thread your needle, Aline?"

The servant replied that she didn't need anyone's help. She fumbled for a long time before she found the eye with her thread. "My hands are no longer steady," she thought.

Catherine told herself it was undoubtedly just as well, nothing could happen, neither happiness nor sorrow, if she remained stationary under the trees, guarded by the servant. Suddenly, the rasping sound of tearing cloth made her start and wince.

"My God, Aline, what are you doing?"

"This sheet is only good for ripping. How pitiful, really, this rented linen is! I, who have known fine faultless linen embroidered with monogrammes."

Catherine had stood up.

"Be quiet, Aline, you're setting my teeth on edge with this terrible tearing of cloth!"

"Such a sad, twisted, little face, just because of the noise of cloth being ripped. Madame is really nervous today."

Catherine moved towards Aline, slowly articulating her words in a hardening voice.

"What an old witch you are, Aline. But all this will be to no avail. I'll leave you when I want, just as I left my husband."

Then she lifted her head quickly towards the olive trees.

"The song of the cicadas!"

Her voice rang out as if announcing a plague of grasshoppers or a storm.

The servant put her hands over her ears, exclaiming, "That was a cursed song," dropped her sheet on the grass and began to hobble painfully down the laneway, an old stubborn goat dragging her age through the parching day.

Catherine stayed late in the garden, not daring to move, holding her breath like someone submitting herself to a futile test.

At dinner, Catherine ate meagrely, hurriedly, under Aline's piercing eye. Then she climbed the stairs, dressed, and arranged her hair very carefully.

With her hair pulled back from her temples and swept up off her neck and the sheen of her skin intensifying the dull violet shadows of her blue dress, Catherine stared at the woman posed before her in the mirror. She recalled the little, uncultivated girl she had been when Michel had taken her and set her to ripen in his closed rooms.

"Is Madame going for a walk?"

Aline had come up without a sound. Catherine swung around. The servant retreated a step, turned her head away, murmuring painfully, almost fearfully: "Madame is too beautiful."

"Look straight at me, Aline, please, and say that again."

"Madame is too beautiful, it cannot last . . ."

"Touch me, Aline, I'm alive and it will last as long as God wills it!"

She grasped the old, knotty, trembling hands between her own, laying them on her cheeks, her forehead, her eyelids. The hard hands lingered on Catherine's forehead, which for that second was girded by a narrow, iron crown.

Catherine spoke in rapid sentences like a volley of stones.

"Don't worry, Aline, I'm going to the seashore. Just for a walk on the pier. Don't bother waiting up for me this evening. It would be better for you to get some rest."

She lifted her hand in a gesture of friendship which froze in mid air. The servant watched her fixedly, without reproach or anger or forgiveness or any signs of life, enclosed in her solitude, her face dead, clinging to her bones.

Catherine left without shutting the door.

The presence of the servant stayed with Catherine for awhile, intermingling with the fragrance of damp gardens. And then there was the boardwalk by the sea, with its strollers. She leaned on the parapet. Bruno came up to her.

"Do you mind if I join you?"

Catherine replied, "No," adding that she would be glad to walk for a little while.

They walked for a long time side by side, sometimes losing, then finding each other in the crowd, like dancers repeating a pattern. They walked without stopping. The cafés, the dance halls, the open-air music halls melted into a noisy, brightly coloured dream.

There were fewer and fewer people. Bruno and Catherine entered the old part of town. Along the narrow, arched streets, smells and voices rose here and there as they passed, from a stream or from a window where laundry hung. Catherine was startled by a small white donkey that rushed towards her at the corner of an alley, clacking its metal hooves, its thin knees wobbling with each step, so laden down with vegetables, fruits and flowers it looked like a huge, bushy bouquet.

The lights were going out one by one. With each step, the young people were in danger of tripping over a stair or a culvert. Here and there, dogs were baying. Bruno walked in front. Catherine tried to keep up. Their main concern in the night was to avoid brushing each other, as if they were two sleep-walkers whom the least shock would hurl into a void.

They arrived at a café where a light was shining. The door was closed. It was opened for them and they were served bread, cheese, wine and two pitiful little peaches. Bruno tore at the bread hungrily, gulped the wine in great draughts, half-closing his eyes. Catherine, ravenously hungry and thirsty, followed suit. Someone said that it was two o'clock. Catherine vaguely heard the patron offering Bruno a room for the night. The young man asked whether they were far from the sea. The patron pointed out the way and led them to the door by the light of a lantern.

"I'm tired," said Catherine, lying down on the

cool, damp pebbles. Bruno stretched out beside her. The strident song of the sea swept over their prone bodies, exposing them, vulnerable and weary, after each ebbing wave.

They waited for daybreak. Bruno asked Catherine if she loved her husband. She shook her head, fascinated by the pallor, the dry lips, the beautiful ravaging thirst overpowering the man's face that was bent over her. Bruno abruptly said that he was free, that he loved Catherine and he wanted her to be his wife.

Catherine turned her head away, murmuring in a barely audible voice that he was asking more than she could give. A sort of rage welled up in her, drowning all tenderness. "It could have been so simple between us. Why must this man speak of love and marriage? So unreasonable. All or nothing. It will be his fault."

Bruno's obstinate voice went on to say that there hadn't been many certain things in his life, but he knew how to recognize the truth. And his hand gently touched Catherine's face, as if it were the most astonishing thing in the world.

Abruptly, she pulled herself away. "As long as I don't tremble," she murmured to herself, all the while assuring Bruno that it was time to go back and that she wasn't interested in becoming attached to anyone.

They walked as far as the olive trees. Catherine fumbled over the good-byes, avoiding Bruno's hands, his eyes, the very sound of his hoarse voice.

Catherine hurried straight up to her room, abandoning her shawl on the stairs where it fell. She tried to tiptoe by the servant's door, determined to see nothing, hear nothing, except the tumult of her own life. "I have only time for happiness," she was thinking.

The servant was calling Catherine in the deep, plaintive voice of a furious and wounded animal. Catherine went into the room. Aline, half collapsed in an armchair, was panting, trying desperately to tear off her linen collar with her right hand. Catherine loosened the black bodice.

"My God, Aline, what's the matter?"

The servant complained of pains in her arms and lack of air. Catherine flung open the window. She kept repeating, "You must lie down, Aline, you must lie down right away. I'll help you and then I'll go fetch a doctor."

In vain she tried to slip a pillow under Aline's hard and heavy head. She was wondering despairingly how she could get help immediately for this old woman who might die. She cried, "Wait, Aline, wait, I beg you. I'll be right back!"

She rushed down the stairs and through the house, turning on all the lights as she passed, although it was already broad daylight. Once in the garden, she gathered a handful of gravel, sought out Bruno's window and hurled her pebbles like a volley of hailstones.

Catherine and Bruno watched over the servant for two days and two nights.

Sometimes Aline angrily pushed away Catherine's hand. But a second later her eyes closed like a corpse and, whimpering softly, she let herself be lifted up by Bruno while Catherine changed the pillows. Catherine was amazed by the sureness and tenderness of Bruno's movements. She was grateful to him for delaying his departure.

They stayed by the servant's bedside for hours at a time without speaking, attentive to her weak breathing as it faltered and then rallied in her battle against enveloping death. In the night, they took turns, each snatching a bit of sleep in the other's warmth in Catherine's bed.

When the doctor had told the servant that her heart was very bad, she answered that it had always been that way, no one had known about it and it concerned nobody but herself. She told how her heart was suffocating in the broad daylight, like her life's burden that she had grimly kept hidden. She now spoke of it freely with the terrible licence of the dying.

"My heart has known much hardship, that's all I can say," she murmured, then moaned as if in a dream how all the masters had betrayed her by their lack of grandeur. "The first master ravished me when I was thirteen. He put me to work under his wife who hated me. Every night he woke me up and took me. The house is as deep as a tomb; no one knows what happens there. Michel and Lia, little ones, little ones, my poor lambs, sleep in peace. Your father is all powerful, your mother is beautiful, little ones, little ones, little ones . . ."

Catherine tried to calm her but Aline furiously pushed her away. "That last great lady in whom I believed, Catherine, Catherine, is false like all the rest, she's a trollop, like Lia, like Madame, her mother, my lords, a real little trollop, and a workman's daughter to boot!"

Catherine wept, her head in her hands.

The servant weakened moment by moment in her sleep, as if she were about to die, then she woke up, calling softly to the little girl she had borne who had been torn from her, "Marie, Marie," she cried.

Catherine and Bruno were then able to give her something to drink and to bathe her face. Dripping with sweat and weeping, she let herself be nursed. Then violently she refused to go to Paradise to serve God, the Virgin and the saints. "I've finished my service, release me, please release me."

She called out again, "Marie, Marie!" Catherine drew near, kissed a cheek already smooth as death. Aline looked up at Catherine, murmured again "Marie"; her face lit up for a moment as if her daughter had been restored to her and she died.

All the flowers in both gardens were cut and offered up to the servant. Pale and swarthy local women dressed in black came to pray over Aline's body. Veiled in their mantillas, they followed the procession in the sun, behind Catherine and Bruno, to the church, then to the cemetery.

This was how the old town carried its dead, under the searching sun, through the maze of narrow, steep streets, then beyond the walls to the top of the mountain. And the dead, buried on the crest of land in the violent heart of the sun, upright like spears in that narrow, rocky space so reminiscent of an altar stone, entreated the thunder of the heavens in behalf of the living.

Catherine took advantage of Bruno's absence to tidy up the servant's room. Among the starched aprons, dresses and worn underwear she found some letters which she tied into a bundle to be burned. Two photographs slid onto the floor. Catherine bent over to pick them up. In one of the photos, she made out the massive silhouette of the seigniorial manor.

In the foreground stood a young man with delicate features, dressed in hunting clothes. Catherine examined that face, which could have been Michel's reduced to its essential hardness but lacking the equivocal softness of tears. "His father," she thought, "how Michel resembles him!" In the other photo she recognized Aline with her protruding eyes, a chubby little girl in a maid's uniform, with two short braids jutting like horns from her fluted bonnet.

Catherine, bent over the photograph, tried for a moment to make out the interior of the hallway behind the little servant framed against the open door. "Everything is black," she thought, recalling the country of Michel and Lia's childhood from which she had escaped like a blind mole digging its passage towards the light.

She was roused from her reverie by Bruno's voice calling her from the garden. She did not answer right away, letting his voice grow surprised, repeating: "Catherine, where are you?" Shouldn't this uncultivated man who had shared these last days of illness and mourning with her learn from Catherine's silence about the secret part of her that was sometimes haunted by the desolate shadow of wood-panelled rooms?

She wrapped all the servant's things up into a parcel, but not knowing what to do with them, remained standing, a big bundle in her hand, vague and lost as in a train station.

"Catherine, where are you?"

His voice was fading away under the trees. She went to the window and called his name. He climbed up, took the parcel from her hands and laid it on a chair. She burst into tears. He pulled her gently by the hand.

"Come, Catherine, come. You mustn't stay here in this room of death."

He led her to the olive trees, made her sit down on the grass and sat beside her.

"What are you going to do now, Catherine?"

Catherine was silent, thinking that she should write Michel and tell him about the servant's death. She was imagining Michel in all his emptiness, re-animated for a moment by the grandeur of the news, tracking down the bitter poetry of death like a quarry, then at once retreating, his own invisible grief revived.

Bruno thought Catherine was brooding about the servant. "Catherine," he murmured, "there's no more you can do for the dead, let the dead worry about the dead."

Catherine looked in amazement at the calm face of this naïve man at her side, speaking so lightly of the merciless truth. "Bruno!" she cried out, as if in a nightmare. The young man took Catherine's head in his hands, gazing at her with a sort of sad eagerness. Catherine told him that she wasn't brave, that her heart had never decided anything on its own, that she had been given a new lease on life and that she constantly needed to feel the earth existing under her and through her. And while she spoke, her fingers caressed Bruno's hands, his shoulder and his cheek with little timid movements. She went on to say that Michel was unhappy, that he loved his sister Lia and that she would never return to them.

157

She also spoke about the job she'd have to find on her return.

"That's for you to decide, Catherine; as for me, I'd very much like you to be my wife . . ."

He had become confused, addressing her in a familiar tone. Catherine despised his bewildered air and wanted to mark that patient face, to brand his likeness to a wounded bull on his low forehead. With both her hands she drew his head towards her.

They decided to stay together until his departure the following day.

He spoke at length about his work. Catherine understood that Bruno's job was to raise and lower by hand the level of rivers. She was pleased with that.

Bruno burned thyme in the servant's room. He took Catherine shopping. On their return, he settled her in the middle of the room with all the provisions within easy reach, worried lest anything was missing. He also gave her some small, bitter lemons. violet sea urchins and wild berries.

Catherine described the delicious strawberries of the north, so unlike any fruit of this baked land. "Nothing ties me any more to Michel," she thought, "and if I'm committing any injustice, it's towards this man here. How can I repay his generosity simply with my delight in being with him, among living things?"

They left the stone house, with its dairy-like coolness. They repeated their summertime rituals, walking side by side on the pebbles among the primitive people of the seashore. They swam together. Bruno licked the salt from Catherine's ankle. Then, once again, silence, the slow fading of light over their reclining brown bodies.

She fixed her hair, crouched on her heels with Bruno facing her, holding the mirror. Then she slipped on her skirt, pulling it up over her feet like a clumsy child.

The dinner was cooking, and smelled delicious. Catherine went up to her room, changed the sheets and arranged some flowers on the chest of drawers. She came back into the living room.

"How serious everything is suddenly!" she thought, setting bread, salt and wine on the table while Bruno stood on the doorstep, his head high, seemingly oblivious to all but the scarcely audible trill of a nightingale lost in the mountains.

The room faced the sea. The large French window was clattering in the wind. Everything smelled of floor polish and clean laundry. Catherine stood by the window, erect and elegant. Bruno came to her, pulled her by her hands gently towards the bedroom. He lifted her onto the bed as one might carry a dying child.

He sought her with his hands and lips, beneath her clothes and her elaborately dressed hair. She spoke of the wind and the sea and turned upon her side, her hair tumbling down in one long cascade. Bruno loved the slight body, painstakingly seeking delight in spots browned by the sun, in tender places of snow or moss with their secret scents.

The violet dawn was gliding along the black tree-trunks and the grey leaves. The olive trees in the field were swaying at the mercy of the wind on their dark and weathered columns. The grass still slept under the dew. Catherine and Bruno went outside slowly, clinging to each other. They were going to part that morning, under the trees, while the cocks crowed at almost regular intervals.

Not a word passed their dry lips, not a sign illumined their blank foreheads. Reluctantly, they detached themselves. For a moment they stood apart, heads lowered, under the olive trees, like solitary monks bowing to each other. They could not speak. Catherine sensed that this man was awaiting a signal from her that could change both their lives, but her heart was knotted in her chest. A voice repeated inside her, "It's up to you to decide, Catherine!"

Suddenly a jubilant chorus of roosters rang out like the crash of brass and it seemed to Catherine and Bruno that they were being pierced by the very cry of a world being born.

Again, the chorus resumed still closer, in shrill unison, so close that it seemed to be perched upon their shoulders. "I'm trembling!" thought Catherine and it was as if the heart of the earth had summoned her to surrender.

She moved towards Bruno, touched his shoulder and murmured softly against his chest that she truly wanted to become his wife.

Catherine was wearing a travelling coat, smart gloves, and a hat which cast a shadow over her eyes. She climbed up the flights of stairs. The odour from the wood-panelled rooms already gripped her at the threshold. She rang the doorbell as if she were a stranger. They took their time answering. Silence buzzed through the oak door like a lost insect. The brass had tarnished, the doorknob and doorbell were already green and blue. There was a sudden movement within and a precipitate clatter of high heels towards the door. Then, once again, silence. Catherine felt that a snarling dog was sniffing at her through the door. She said: "It's me, Catherine."

There was a muffled exclamation, then an unsteady hand pulled the bolt and opened the door. Lia leaned on the door frame like someone afraid of falling. She looked at Catherine without seeing her, repeating in her contained voice: "Catherine, Catherine, really, this isn't possible."

"May I come in, I'd like to see Michel?"

Lia slowly stepped aside to let Catherine pass. It took two tries before she could close the door.

Right away Catherine noticed that things were fallen, displaced, dirty and scattered. And suddenly, in the way one sometimes isolates a motif in a complicated abstract design, she recognized, amid the chaos of the room, an order peculiar to Lia and Michel, a sort of encampment set up on the rug by the corner of the fireplace, a circle of dirty glasses and ashtrays overflowing with butts around an open book.

"We were reading," said Michel, by way of excuse.

"It's of no importance," added Lia.

She kicked the book shut and left the room trying to do up her hair, which was falling down in great tangles while pins kept dropping onto the floor.

Catherine and Michel were left alone. Catherine drew near and seized Michel's wrist as if grabbing a wandering child.

"Listen to me, Michel, please."

Michel was neither looking at nor listening to Catherine. He said with a sort of mournful ecstasy,

"We were reading, it's the first time since Lia's return..."

Catherine informed him that the servant had died, and that she was in love with another man. She wanted her freedom, she told him. Michel listened to her distractedly, as if she were one of those story-tellers who babble on through long evenings. Then he started to tell her about Lia's last escapade.

Just then, Lia came back into the room, her damp hair sticking to her shoulders, her gaunt chastened body conspicuous through her clinging nightgown. She said, "I'm going to bed," and slammed the door behind her. Michel spoke in a low, terrified voice, "She came back this morning, her colouring ashes, angry, robbed, starved, wounded in the shoulder. Now she's sleeping. She'll be like that for days and nights on end, lying there uncovered, apparently without dreaming, like a dried-up corpse thown across the bed."

"Tell me about yourself, Michel."

"About me, Catherine? There's nothing worth telling, I assure you. I've spent agonizing days, waiting, in shame. But I know she always comes back; it's stronger than she is. We fast and we pray together. One day, I think, she'll become as pure again as her bones. We'll renew the pact of our childhood and no one will reach us."

He had raised his voice. He was looking at Catherine without seeing her, seeming to defy someone behind her.

"My poor Michel, how bitter all this is. Look at me a little, because I'm going to leave you forever."

Michel turned quickly towards Catherine, appearing to notice her for the first time.

"Ah! Catherine, how you've changed! You look like a grand lady on a visit and you trouble me. Why that hat, those gloves? How elegant you are, how beautiful and cruel."

Catherine took off her hat and gloves. She unbuttoned her coat and stood before Michel, concealing nothing, neither the fullness of her figure, the roundness of her cheeks, nor the plenitude of the joy that spread over her skin like a nasturtium in bloom. Michel covered his eyes with his hands and reproached Catherine for the shamelessness of her life.

"What a wounded little girl I lost along the way," he kept repeating, "and who will keep me company during Lia's heavy sleep?"

"Kiss me, Michel, because I'm going to leave for good."

Michel kissed Catherine's cheek fearfully. His fingers stroked her tanned arm. Catherine submitted patiently and with pity to this stranger's light touch.

"Here is the ring, Michel, the ring you gave me."

And she put it in his hand.

Michel looked with astonishment at the gold ring lying in the hollow of his open palm.

"But what will I do with this ring, Catherine?"

Catherine was silent. She closed her eyes for a moment, gathering up her past like someone on the verge of death, and, unable to separate it from Michel's strange gifts, discovered there a poem he had taught her and replied: "A very tiny ring for the dream, Michel, only a very tiny ring."